THE
SENTIMENTAL
ASSASIN

SAM W. ANDERSON

Published by
ROTHCO PRESS
1331 Havenhurst Drive #103
West Hollywood, CA 90046

Cover Design: Rob Cohen

Rothco Press is a division of Over Easy Media Inc.
www.RothcoPress.com
@RothcoPress

The Sentimental Assassin by Sam W. Anderson
Paperback ISBN: 978-1-945436-30-7
Ebook ISBN: 978-1-945436-31-4

Fiction: Thriller; Fiction: Mystery/Detective

THE SENTIMENTAL ASSASIN

SAM W. ANDERSON

ROTHCO PRESS • LOS ANGELES, CALIFORNIA

For Mom and, always, Nichelle

In Memory of Larry Meier

Introduction

That endless black ribbon means lonesome...
Tombstone every mile...

I was raised in the mountains of Pennsylvania. Reared on hard rock and country/gospel. Stealing my Pap's trucker tapes to play in a shitty portable cassette player out in the shed while I snooped through boxes of junk. Red Simpson and Red Sovine along with Dick Curless and Jimmy Martin helped me create a wonderful imaginative world where big rigs roamed the highways like dinosaurs. And once I made it to adulthood and had long ago forsaken the daydream and child's play, I still adored this music. truck driving music is a form like no other. I tell you all this to pave the way for the next bit so belly up and be patient.

All of that was shelved away in my brain. I mean, I still dug music of all flavors but hadn't even thought of trucker music in probably twenty years or more. I was excitedly working with Ken Wood, Nick Contor and Mercedes Yardley on a new horror fiction publication called *Shock Totem*, when fate would have a review copy of Sam W. Anderson's *American Gomorrah* cross my path. I dug in blindly and I'm not exaggerating when I say it profoundly changed me.

Sam, with his *Money Run* series, has taken all the over-the-top characters of a Lansdale novel and throw them into a world of truck stops and big rigs. We've got human trafficking and drug trade. We've got hookers and hallucinations. Things both natural and supernatural and it's all played as though it's just the way the world spins. I fucking love that.

After delivering that omnibus of his *Money Run* stories, Sam gave us another novel, *The Nines*, which was more pedal-to-the-metal batshit road-set chaos. By the time I finished this one I knew I was a fan for life. I knew Anderson was a writer whom I would follow into the fire of Hell if asked to. His output, while not frequent, is always the stuff of quality. I mean, quality if you're up for his brand of bizarre road movie as directed by David Lynch and Tarantino after they got drunk on moonshine kinda material. So yeah, I'm saying it's amazing!

I say all of that so I can say this about his latest,*The Sentimental Assassin*. This one is a doozy! It's truckier than a Walmart parking lot and has more firepower than an NRA member's wet dream.

Much like the predecessors, this one has ties the *Money Run*. But it plays at almost a different speed, one that showcases Sam's rich talent for painted wonderfully wild characters. It's brimming with enough action to make John Rambo light-headed. It's so much damned fun.

I'm not the greatest at writing a focused introduction to a book I dug. I am good at being honest and calling it like I see it. I see Sam W. Anderson breaking it big very soon. Hell, it's long overfuckingdue...but if you fancy yourself a fan of road movies...

If hearing "Slow Ride" makes you smile...

If you like to wear leather even when it's 80 degree outside.

If you like the feel of the gear shifting and the hum of the road under your tires.

Honey, this one's for you. Sit back and buckle up... this one is bumpy in all the right way.

Roll out.

– John Boden (Author of *Walk the Darkness Down* and *Jedi Summer*)

The scope of *The Money Run*, the power it wields, the financial impact it generates, puts its clandestine status in constant jeopardy. Certain "outside" groups know parts of its existence, but the concept of The Run seems too grand for mainstream America to take such rumors seriously (and it's in the general citizenry's interest to simply turn a convenient, blind eye). Most groups in the know are little threat to The Money Run itself. Most. But that brings us to the PAGANS...

– Excerpt from *The Money Run: American Gomorrah* by James Phizer

February, 2013. In the middle of fucking nowhere:

Let there be no question: Jo Martindale was not trans. She held no interest in being nor becoming male and only wore men's clothes because her wife, while she'd been alive, had claimed Vanilla Ice would make one damn-fine looking lesbian. Abigail said it often in death, too.

"Nineties Vanilla Ice," she'd tell Jo in the dreams brought on by the various anesthesias administered over the years. "Before the facial hair. I don't dig girls with facial hair." This despite the gray stray strands that had hung from Abigail's own chin. "I got standards," she'd say from a million miles away.

This mission, though, the story of this story, would bring Jo closer to her beloved Abs in some manner. Either she'd use the bounty Deacon Rice had offered to finance another plastic surgery – one to square off her own hairless chin and improve upon her Vanilla Icyness – or she'd meet her soul mate on the other side. Either way, she'd be cool. Either fucking way.

The blood-red Plymouth Duster, three on the tree and factory eight track intact, kept at a steady fifty over the snow-crunched, one-lane road. UFO's *Lights Out* screamed full blast on a continuous loop. Had been since Jo'd bought the muscle car from Deacon Rice some two years earlier with the volume dial already missing in action. Jo'd never heard a single note, though. Felt them. All of the ever-loving benevolent bass beats that vibrated through the driver-seat cracked vinyl and jetted up and down her spine. Kept her moist. Reminded her of more musical times. Over the months, she'd grown so accustomed to the constant thumping, Jo didn't know if she could operate the Duster without "Too Hot to Handle" pulsing through her thighs.

Outside, moonbeams and headlights met the snow blanketing the vast oil fields, creating an eerie grayish hue. The mechanical donkey pumpers looked like enormous prehistoric birds, somehow motorized as they bobbed and sucked up the black goo from their long-gone ancestors rotting several strata beneath the Dakota plains.

Jo removed the night-vision specs dangling from the gearshift and cut the headlights before adjusting the goggles into place. Although she'd been assured surprise sided with her, Jo wanted to maintain that advantage. Any advantage. Especially considering her target, and Jo didn't much care to consider her target.

On the horizon, the shed appeared. Smoke wisped from a cylindrical metal chimney, and the light from the sole window appeared like a firefly frozen in place over the snow-covered horizon. Jo's stomach tightened and tumbled. She wished she could fast forward through the following few hours as no possible outcome appeared palatable. She understood part of her soul would die in that damn shed. Scenarios played in her mind, horrific possibilities with once-loved ones dead and body parts missing. She gnashed and ground and gritted her teeth.

She never saw the road spikes. Never heard, of course, the Goodyears blow.

The Duster fishtailed before the flat front tires found the small, snakelike ravine bordering the road. Jo's seatbelt locked. The first roll popped the perpetually stuck UFO eight-track tape free. The second broke off the passenger door. The several that followed tossed the Duster's contents – a practical trash bin of fast-food wrappers and spent steroid syringes mingled with a shit-ton of extra ammo – with tornadic force. By the time the car came to a rest on its top, the music had stopped vibrating through Jo. Instead, she endured the assorted contusions from the seatbelt constraints, the agony from when her elbow had cracked against the door, and the concussion – mild as it was – still a beautiful, fresh brain bruise piled atop the past collection so vast, she'd grown to enjoy the experience. The belt pinned and hung her upside-down in her seat with blood rushing to her woozy head. She began a quick inventory of her weapons, but couldn't get past the idea that maybe she'd punctured one of the propane tanks in her breastplate. She smelled no hint nor tint of the fetid fuel in the frigid harsh air, though.

The crash had played out in a silent, sublime scene for her, but the crunching metal had surely alerted anybody holed up in the shed. Jo re-adjusted her goggles and depressed the seatbelt latch. The constraint gave no quarter. Tugging and twisting yielded no results, either. She dangled, suspended like a helpless fly trapped and awaiting the famished spider. Well, as helpless of a fly as a world-class, take-no-sass, kick-you-and-your-mama's-ass assassin could possibly be.

The light inside the shed went dark.

Jo needed to cut herself free, pronto, and reached for the knife in her boot only to find the sheath empty. Her heart thundered beneath the propane tits. A conglomeration of extra ammo clips and smaller caliber guns lay scattered across the crumpled car ceiling, and Jo probed through the mess, searching for her missing knife.

I can't do this, she thought. Even if she could, she couldn't. Through the concussion fog, a notion nagged at her about how she should've easily freed herself. She somehow knew the answer was so obvious, it taunted her just behind conscious thought. She couldn't find it, though, and the harder she searched for the fleeting idea, the further away it scurried.

In the snow, Jo's target crept closer. The body outline displayed by the goggles, the size and grace with which it moved, allowed no doubt: Polly approached. A military-style weapon rested against her shoulder, aimed at the Duster. Through the weapon's scope, Polly, Jo's once-sweet Polly, watched on as Jo struggled against the Duster's seatbelt. The infra-red blur of Polly's figure brought back the past with a wallop of nuclear might. Seeing her approach upside-down added to the surreal sense of the scene.

Blood drained heavily into Jo's head and weighed against her sinuses and useless ears. Her head was a lava lamp, each thought a blob breaking from the amalgamation filling her skull.

Polly hastened her pace, still watching Jo through the scope.

Jo fought the malaise and, in desperation, grasped a .22 caliber semi-auto from the array strewn overhead. She aimed. She aimed so fucking hard.

In response, Polly unstrapped her weapon and dropped it. She burst into full sprint, awkward against the knee-deep day-old snow. She waved her hands over her head, obviously yelling despite the futility inherent in the act.

Still, Jo kept the pistol on her target. She bit back the emotions tormenting her. C'mon Jo, she thought. You're a pro's pro – a hardcore bitch. She's making it easy on you. Just take the fucking shot and go collect your damn money.

Polly's pace slowed, the snow clearly sapping her energy, but she trudged forward. She drew close enough that Jo took the goggles off and still easily saw her quarry in the moonlight. If it'd been any other alive and real person, Jo would have dropped her, a clean headshot because Polly surely had draped herself in Kevlar. And maybe, if that was all the job required, she'd have finished it right there. Probably not, but she'd like to have thought she would have.

Jo lowered the gun. "I'm gonna do this the hard way, aren't I?"

When Polly finally arrived at the destroyed Duster, she almost danced in circles, a puppy greeting its master after a long and tortuous separation. However, a scarf covered Polly's mouth so Jo couldn't read her lips. Jo simply stared at her former lover's almond-shaped eyes and thought: The really fucking hard way. This damn Asian fetish is going to get me killed someday.

It took several moments before Polly seemed to realize all her babbling was for naught. She stumbled through the snow and rubble, around to the missing passenger-side door and crawled through the clutter covering the ceiling. The joy previously evident in her eyes faded, overtaken by an unmistakable melancholy. Slowly, she reached for the red scarf covering her face and pulled it down.

"It's true then?"

"What?" Jo found it a bit difficult reading Polly's lips upside down.

"That cocksucker took your hearing?" At least that's what Jo thought Polly had said. It could have been "earring," but that made little sense. Tear swelled in Polly's eyes. "He made you motherfucking deaf?"

"Not exactly. I mean...it's kind of a long story."

Polly leaned and kissed Jo lightly. Jo would have smiled, but all the plastic surgeries had resulted in nerve damage that left the gesture a part of her perpetual past.

"I barely recognized you. I mean, I knew it was you when I saw the Duster, but you hardly look at all like..." Polly said. "Except for the eyes. They're still you." She smoothed her fingers over the bridge of Jo's nose. "I like this, though. Makes you look less like a ruffian."

"I am a motherfucking ruffian."

Polly pulled up Jo's red leather coat sleeve and revealed the "Yo Ma-Ma" tattoo on the inside forearm. The words were scripted in cursive, made to look like the bridge of a cello, and were bracketed by F holes – those squiggly "s" shapes common on orchestral string instruments. Four lines, each of the proper thickness, represented the strings, and intersected the lettering. "That's still you, too." She kissed Jo again. "But that's about all."

"Yeah, you might say I've had a little work done." Then Jo looked at the tattoo with a little regret, like always, and remembered how she could've cut herself free. She decided to keep the info to herself, though – no need for Polly to see the full arsenal just yet.

"A little work? And the Kardashians slightly enjoy a smidgen of attention now and then."

"And you're still a smart-ass."

"And you're queer." (Maybe "here?" Upon reflection, Jo thought that more likely.) Polly kissed her again, a little longer, a little firmer. "I knew that bastard would send you."

"I am the best he has. You should be flattered."

"Honored." Polly reached into her belt and produced a large serrated knife.

Jo grabbed Polly's wrist. "Before you cut me down, you need to know, I'm going to murdalize the shit out of you. It's what I do."

"I know what you do."

"I know you know. I know you saw it in me. That's why you sought me out back in Maxville, wasn't it?"

Polly said something and began sawing at the seatbelt. From the angle, Jo couldn't read her lips. Somehow she understood she'd end up paying for that. Somehow, she didn't care. She settled in for what would surely be one of the longest nights of her life.

The elbow Polly delivered knocked Jo's ass right the fuck out.

# # #

May, 2006. The start of it all in the Heartland:

In rural Iowa, Maxville to be exact, an out lesbian was as rare as a post-graduate degree. Yet there stood Jo. Behind the counter of the Woolworth's soda fountain where one couldn't tell if it was 1956 or 2006 – except for Jo's pierced tongue and the trophy residing on the counter: 2005 District Champ, Wrestling. Jo Marindale (sic), 135 Pounds. Jo had explained for Polly the counter's manager wanted the trophy there. Something about making the local yokels feel more comfortable about a lesbian serving them their sodas and fries without passing on the gay gene. It made as much sense as it sounded.

Polly had pegged Jo a possible PAGANS right away – an outsider harboring an honest anger simmering just beneath the surface, fiery enough to warm the air surrounding her, and needing a life-changing orgasm like a lung required air. Over the prior two weeks, Polly had embarked on recruitment – a seduction on many levels, and a skill Polly thought herself well-versed in – but Jo had rebuffed her at every turn. On this unusually hot, typically sticky day, Polly had had enough of that shit.

"Yo, bitch!" Polly said in some attempt to break Jo's disinterest. A failed attempt as the waitress responded in no fashion. Polly slid her half-empty coffee cup down the lunch counter in a grand gesture. Unabated, it glided the length of the lipstick-red Formica, over the lip and smashed onto the faded-black and dull-white checkerboard-tiled floor with a clatter.

Jo didn't bother turning her head and focused on wiping down that same bar, mouthing the lyrics to whatever song played on her iPod. A hairnet trapped her pink hair, and the uniform – a nondescript yellow dress and bleached apron – did little for her athletic body. Her face was angelic except for the nose which must have been broken several times to achieve such angles. A button affixed to the uniform apron read: "I'm not vegetarian, I eat pussy." She refused to return Polly's stare, and Polly wanted her more than ever. For PAGANS. For herself.

Polly reached across the counter and yanked the ear buds. The Ramones' *Blitzkrieg Bop* rang out in tinny tones. The glare Jo fired back might have killed a lesser person, and considering Jo'd once shared that she held a fourth degree black belt in karate, the idea wasn't so far-fetched.

"Can I get another cup of coffee?"

"Can you suck my motherfucking dick?"

Polly laughed despite herself. "Bucking for employee of the month, are we?"

"Look, Stalky McBitchpants," Jo re-inserted the headphone into her left ear, but let the right one dangle, the song emerging from it as if performed by a flea circus. "I don't care what you want, but the answer is unequivocally, indubitably and totally and always: 'no.'"

"What if I wanted to give you a gazillion dollars?"

"You have a gazillion dollars?" Jo grabbed another mug from the wire rack under the counter and filled it with the greasy brew that passed as coffee.

"No, but--"

"This is my last shift, lady. I told you, summer semester starts in two weeks. I don't know why you come in every day, and yeah, I'm a little flattered, but can't a girl spend her last working day in relative peace? No complications, no problems, and pardon my manners, but you got 'problems' written all over you."

Polly nodded. Knew she wasn't letting Jo off that easily, but nodded anyway.

The bell above the entrance jangled and Polly jumped, reflexively reaching for the .22 in her ankle holster before catching herself. Jo winked, letting her know the action hadn't gone unnoticed.

"Morning, Walter," Jo said.

"Morning, Lezzy Jo." The octogenarian shuffled to the bar. Blue suspenders struggled to hold up Wranglers over his considerable belly and his grease-stained ball cap advertised some farm equipment company. "My order ready?"

Jo produced a Styrofoam to-go box and a large paper coffee cup from beneath the counter. Before grabbing a handful of napkins, she opened the box so Walter could confirm the pie was apple. Polly saw no evidence of the loogie Jo had deposited atop the slice when she'd taken the phone order.

The old man took his to-go bag and tipped his cap because he was a gentleman. "You and your girlfriend cunt have a good day."

When the bell rang again upon his exit, Polly startled despite anticipating the clanging.

"Yeah, you're not up to anything," Jo said. "You're jumpier than Wesley Snipes at an IRS inquiry."

"Never claimed I wasn't up to something."

"You smell like trouble to me." Jo took an actual sniff. "And tequila."

"You smell like a fantasy."

In response, Jo released a god-awful, ten-second fart, wet and loose and cringe inducing. "That part of your fantasy?"

Polly took the gesture as some sort of odd compliment. If Jo felt that comfortable around her, then maybe the work of the past couple weeks had taken root. "You still going off to that music school then?"

"That music school. Julliard. Same fucking thing, I suppose."

Polly popped one of the plastic Half-and-Half containers, aiming the contents at the coffee cup. "You're going to leave all this behind, huh?" What the 'rents have to say?"

"The 'rents?"

"Yeah. Ma and Pa...you know. Don't the kids say 'the 'rents' anymore?"

"Did kids ever say 'the 'rents?'" With mop in hand, Jo strolled around the counter to clean the mess from Polly's first cup. "The 'rents think they're not going to have to deal with their dyke-ass daughter anymore, and everybody in town will love Pastor and Mrs. Martindale again. Shit – they hightailed it to Des Moines earlier this week. Not too fond of farewells, I guess."

"And they going to love you at Julius? How's the wrestling team there?"

"It's Julliard." Jo left the mop bucket and yellow caution sign by the spill and returned behind the counter.

"I know what it's called – just messing with you." Polly reached into her cleavage, impressive and proudly displayed for Jo's benefit, and removed a wad of cash bigger than a baby's head. She peeled off a Grant and held the rest of the money as if she were about to deal a hand of poker. "Your friends throwing a goodbye party? You all going to the water tower and tip cows in your dungarees, or some shit like that, Josephine?"

"Don't call me that." Jo's glare burrowed into Polly. She let the fifty dollars rest, unloved, on the counter.

"My bad. Polly smirked. "Jo. You and your friends planning on making a night of it?"

"What friends?"

Polly stripped another fifty from the stack. She set it atop its twin on the Formica. "Seriously? No goodbye to Maxville, Jo?" She stressed "Jo" in a sneering sarcastic tone.

"Sneaking out under the cover of dark. Nobody's going to miss me." Jo wouldn't take her eyes from Polly's, as if the cash on the counter didn't exist.

Another bill. "Nobody?" Another. "I'll miss you."

"Can't miss what you never had."

"Never heard of opportunity? I've missed a shit-ton of those. Not planning on missing the one in front of me now, though." Polly tapped at the hanging ear bud, sending it swinging. "Am I a nobody?"

"You're not from here. You're sure as fuck not Maxville."

"No shit. Not much of an Asian contingency in your fair town. Chinese restaurant serves hamburgers, for fuck sake." Polly grabbed a cellophane-wrapped toothpick from the teacup next to the grease-stained napkin holder. "You ain't Maxville, either, are you, Jo?"

Jo allowed a smile and bit her tongue just behind the stud. "If I were anymore Maxville, I'd shit corn husk."

"You should probably see a doctor about that." Polly expected a better reaction to her joke. "You're so Maxville, where's your sendoff?"

"Don't want one. Don't need one. Won't be one."

"Bullshit." Polly dropped another bill on the counter. She hoped it'd do the trick, because the rest of the "bills" were ones and coupons and all she had for the remaining three weeks of the month. Unless she planned on tapping her newfound special reserve, and at that particular point, that particular reserve was just that – she couldn't court Jo properly without it. "I might not be Maxville, but maybe let me send you off the right way?" In one, too-quick-for-the-eye motion, she reinserted the remaining cash and coupons in her bra, popped the toothpick from its wrapper and flipped it in her mouth as she produced a business card for Jo. The card was from the auto body shop, but Polly'd lined through everything in black ball-point pen and had written her RV lot number and cell phone on the back. Around the information, she'd drawn a heart. Not a valentine heart, but a human organ. "What time you clock out?"

"After your bedtime, old lady. Maybe four-thirty. P-fucking-M." Jo slid the cash pile across the counter like Polly figured she would. "I'm not exactly onto your game yet, but I don't want your charity."

"I don't give charity, but I believe you should help a friend when you can. Plus, it's always to be good to be in the right side of the ledger when it comes to favors." Polly put her hand over Jo's. F-U-C-K covered Polly's right-hand knuckles, a letter assigned to each finger. "Don't kid yourself, Josephine. New York is an expensive goddamned city. You're going to need that money. But if you want to earn it, I'm down with that, too." She leaned on the counter, arms beneath her tits to inflate them.

Jo reached into her apron pocket for a lighter. She flicked the Bic and held the cash up with her other hand. Polly leaned forward and blew until the flame died. She took the lighter from Jo, who didn't contest the action, and placed it beneath her own bra strap. "You're not that stupid."

"Never underestimate anybody's stupid."

"Smartest advice I've ever heard." Looking into Jo's eyes, Polly realized how bad she needed this recruit. PAGANS existence might well depend on her landing Jo Martindale. "Meet me after work? I'll sit on your face so hard, I'll straighten that nose for you."

Jo turned her head away and stuffed the fifties back into Polly's blouse. Her fingers stayed inside longer than necessary "You should go."

"Not even dinner?" Polly raised her eyebrows in a suggestive manner and cracked a coy smile. "C'mon, Jo. I still have a little left in the tank – I ain't hit thirty yet. You could do a lot worse than dinner with me for a final celebration."

"Yeah, right – dinner. Ever notice in mob movies that before they whack somebody, they almost always have a meal with them first?" She returned to wiping away the nothingness on the counter. "I've worked my whole life to get out of this town. I'm not fucking anything up on the last day. You're not whacking me, Ms. Polly. You're not whacking my plans, either." Jo took Polly's untouched coffee cup and set it in the bussing bin where it clinked against the other dirty dishes. "But you're kind of cute for an old broad, and I have a thing for Asians. Maybe if you'd been a year earlier."

"Ha! Story of my life." Polly sat erect, rapped a quick drumbeat on the counter, spun a three-sixty on the chrome stool and stood. "If you change your mind, I'll be home all night. I'll leave a light on."

She left Woolworth's post haste to properly prepare for her imminent date with Jo. And to initiate her into the PAGANS.

#

Still May 2006. Later that evening. A Caddy and a baddie:

Around the time Polly considered killing the last lamp and sulking out of Iowa's untended asshole defeated, headlights darted through the RV's drapes and danced across the wood paneling. A charge jumpstarted her, and she vibrated with electricity. Showtime! she thought, already as wet as the sea at high tide on a rainy day. Taking one final preparatory glance around, she spotted the half-empty, silver spray-paint container in the wastebasket.

"Well, that was nearly a major fuck up right there." Polly emptied half a tissue box, pulling out each like a cheesy magician tugging an endless stream of hankies from his pants. She buried the can beneath the hefty heap of tissues and tied the grocery-store-bag lining into a knot.

Consciously slowing her gait so not raise Jo's suspicions, she exited the RV and headed for the communal dumpsters just across the way. Her racing heart accelerated even more when she spied the car motoring down the cramped motor-home-park alley. It wasn't Jo's Prius. Instead, some Cadillac Das Boat soft-top sedan straight out of 1975, long as most RVs in the park, crawled toward her. She hadn't seen the car in her two weeks in Maxville, but relaxed a bit when she saw the shadow of a child in the passenger seat. No assassin, not even the pieces of shit Deacon Rice contracted with, would bring a kid on a job. The car neared, and The Brother's Johnson's "Strawberry Letter 23" blared from its stereo, shaking the windows with each bass beat.

Once it crept close enough, the driver's immense size became evident. Polly realized that wasn't any kid in the passenger seat.

She reached for her ankle holster, but she'd discarded it earlier while rubbing one out, lost in fantasy about Jo. Breaking into a sprint, she dove for cover behind the metal dumpsters that reeked of empty alcohol bottles and used diapers.

The tissues camouflaged the spray paint can well – too well – but Polly finally found it after ripping through the plastic bag. The canister clanged when it hit the cracked asphalt, and Polly gathered it before the can skittered into the car's headlight beams.

The Caddy stopped. Somehow, the volume of the song doubled when the doors opened, yet Polly still heard her own thundering heartbeat. Then, like that, the music cut off, leaving the air too loud to listen to.

"Polly olly oxen free."

Polly had never heard the voice before, but deduced who it belonged to immediately. The slight Spanish accent and the high-pitched dwarf tone gave away its owner. It sounded like a member of the Lollypop Guild had broken bad.

"C'mon out, bitch. Let's get this over with."

Polly harbored every intention of coming out, just not yet. She reached into her bra strap.

Footsteps crushed broken glass decorating the alleyway. Slow footsteps, heavy and moving with nefarious purpose. The streetlight backlit shadows, and the size of the big one was un-fucking-natural. Polly'd learned through her years of recon that they grew them big on The Run, though.

Goddamn Money Run anyway.

"Deacon Rice sends his love. Come with us now and I'm sure you two can come to a reasonable accord."

Polly would have rather died a million painful-ass times in a million unimaginable, painful-ass ways than subject herself to one session with that sadistic cocksucker, Rice.

More crushed glass. The shadows swelled, revealing the midget's figure and his missing arm, amputated at the elbow. This confirmed Polly's earlier identification. Based upon PAGANS intelligence, limited as it might have been, she knew she could ill afford to assume size, or the lack there of, provided any advantage over her pursuer. The One-Armed Bandit was one malicious motherfucker by all accounts. A full-fledged superstar on the lucrative Money Run midget tossing circuit, Lefty Gonzales had stood out – for all the wrong reasons – in several PAGANS briefings. Extortion, tenuous ties to a triple murder, heavily involved in the drug trade – all the reasons Polly and the PAGANS pledged to take The Run down. Even if the vigilante group had to lower themselves to such tactics, as well.

One more step, and the two shadows merged. Polly estimated the pair stopped about fifteen feet away. A long toss, no doubt, but based on legends she'd heard, a reasonable distance for The Bandit to inflict some serious damage.

"Last chance, Polly. Come out now and save yourself a shit-ton of pain." The shadows displayed the behemoth driver swinging Lefty Gonzales, holding him by the scruff of his collar and crotch. "We might even take turns instead of double penetration. Probably not, but I'd consider it."

Polly stood, inhaled and emerged from the dumpster's cover. "How can I pass on an offer like that?" Her hands remained behind her back. "Unfortunately, Shortcake, I ain't got two things: Time for your bullshit or something to lose. This ain't your Money Run, ass-wipe. You hunt me on the grid, among The Heat? I scream rape and out here, in the real world, lights go on, dipshit. People come out." Although Polly had endured enough trailer parks to know this not to be the usual case.

"Skip the witty banter, Lefty," the big guy grunted. "You're getting freaking heavy."

"Go ahead and scream, Polly. I think you want to land in a cop shop less than me." Lefty's voice volume raised and lowered as he swung forward and back. "You know Deacon's got somebody on the payroll to clear my ass. How you going to explain yourself?"

Polly sneered, but offered no answer.

The One-Armed Bandit sneered back and raised his stump. "Now!"

"'Bout fucking time," the tosser said between belabored breaths.

Before Polly could process the events, the massive muscular man tossed the menacing midget, arcing him through the yellow streetlight glow, and Lefty released a scream that would elicit pride from a kung-fu movie soundman. He screwed through the air, stump extended. Reaching for the nub, Lefty pumped in a shotgun motion, and a blade appeared with a whoosh like the un-sheathing of a sword.

Polly dove and barrel-rolled, coming to her knees as the street's broken glass bit into her. She held the Bic to the aerosol spray paint can and lit the lighter.

Ignition. An enormous whoosh.

The dwarf sailed past, disappearing into the monstrous fireball that illuminated the entire RV park. Midget screams echoed off tin and aluminum of the trailers. The heat curled paint on the closest dwellings. The inferno lasted only a moment, though. As the aerosol ran out, the flames diminished. Sputtered. And in the wake, the midget rose.

His mullet had been burnt away, steam swirling about his now bald head creating clouds of stinky burnt dwarf, but he appeared unharmed in any other way. Unharmed and pissed. The swastika tattoo between his eyebrows disappeared as he scrunched his face and roared.

"Deacon wanted you alive, but the crazy mother-fucker didn't say how alive." The bandit sprung forward and caught Polly about the thigh with his good arm. The stump swung in an uppercut, blade directed toward Polly's special bits before she blocked with a low kick. The titanium clipped her inner thigh. Blood spurted in a gory crimson gusher.

As she bucked, Lefty sunk his teeth deep into ass cheek. Polly howled. She lost balance. When she landed on the Bandit's head, the crack resonated like a broken walnut, and he released his hold on her leg.

"Lefty!" The earth shook as the Bandit's thrower closed. He was a generic big guy. A lug. An obvious product of The Run – somebody who'd found himself in an environment where only those who couldn't find themselves thrived. But he moved fast – too fast to elude.

The thrower launched, struck Polly beneath the jaw with his shoulder, and she skidded, raw backside bite injury and all, across the alleyway. She yelped as ground beer-bottle remnants burrowed into exposed, spewing wounds. The shards found every tender nerve, and pain danced a tango up her spine and back down again. In stilettos. Acid tipped stilettos.

Polly's head banged against her RV with a deafening thud. Her attacker skidded past, reaching for her ankle as he landed. He caught her with a grip so fierce, she thought he might squeeze her bones to dust.

The lights of the various trailers and RVs went out. Polly feared she would, too.

Cocking her free leg, she stomped into the assailant's nose. The explosion of blood painted his face into a visceral Rorschach blot. A butterfly with horns, Polly thought. Maybe a vagina lit aflame.

The blow only angered the giant, though. Before she could deliver another, he swung her by the leg as if she weighed less than a dust bunny. He struggled to his knees, then his feet, lifting Polly by the ankle and hanging her like a fisherman would display his catch. Her miniskirt draped over her torso and revealed the thong with the Cookie Monster's face on the front. Blood greased her thighs.

Just as he was about to slam her into the ground, a thwack that surely and easily would have finished her, the yell erupted: "Stop!" Backlit by the Caddy headlights, limping, steaming in more than one sense of the word, Lefty Gonzales resembled an animated doll from an eighties' horror movie. "Save some for me."

The midget tosser dropped Polly, her head meeting asphalt first, and she literally saw stars – Madonna, Garbo, Hayworth – blurring in and out of her fading vision. She attempted to sweep the big dude's leg, but her body wouldn't respond to her mind's commands.

It seemed to take forever and a week and a little while longer for the midget to reach her. With each of his tiny steps, another vision of how he'd torture her flashed through Polly's mind. In her discombobulated state, she cackled like a madwoman at the images of a dwarf doing her in.

"Deacon's going to love you, ain't he? Lefty's kick landed square in her ribs. "I understand he's into Chinese food."

"Sorry, Shortcake. I ain't Chinese."

"Who gives a fuck?" He stepped over her, straddled so his crotch situated directly over her face. "Take her inside. Let's teach the bitch what real pain is."

Polly reckoned she'd already learned a lesson or two.

Every nerve in her body screamed in protestation as the Goliath dragged her up the metal stairs and into the Winnebago.

Several minutes later, inside the RV, unconsciousness toyed with her. Whenever it threatened to finally drag her under, Lefty used one of her open wounds as an ashtray, grinding out a grape cigarillo before re-lighting it and starting over again. The torture stank of burnt flesh, cheap tobacco and cheaper wine. Goosebumps formed on her naked skin. She shivered from cold unsuited to the warm night. Shook from exhaustion. She whimpered and waited for the worst to begin.

As Lefty unzipped his pants, his dwarf laugh demonic, the RV's door burst open.

The shadow in the maw held a baseball bat in one hand as something dangled from the other. Polly recognized the object – a cello fingerboard with one tuning peg still intact, one final string pathetically attached to a shattered piece of the instrument's body that swung like a pendulum. The figure elbowed the light switch, revealing Jo in all her glory. Moist mascara trails darkened her cheeks. Her eyes, puffy and smudged, exposed a rage like Polly had never seen. She didn't know if she should be happy to see Jo or not.

Before she could decide, the ginormous midget tosser jumped. He wrapped Jo about the waist, and the two
disappeared outside.

"Looks like we're going to have a full-on orgy, huh
Polly?" Lefty said.

"Not how I'd describe it."

"I didn't ask you."

"You kind of did." She slid her hand underneath the
driver's seat.

Lefty struggled with the button on his junior Levis.
His erection poked his boxers through the open zipper.

Polly found what she searched for among the dried
French fries and lost change. With ninja quickness, she
slung the yard-long, double-headed dildo against the
One-Armed Bandit's temple. The wallop knocked the
dwarf to his knees.

Slipping behind him, Polly shoved him face first into
the rank shag carpet and sat on his back. She reached
under his chin, interlocking her fingers so the "F-U-
C-K" tattoos from one hand meshed with the "D-A-L-E"
from her other hand, and pulled Lefty's head back. His
scream sounded like a siren. Polly shut him up by jamming the purple and green striped sex toy down his gul-
let. The siren morphed into a gagging squeal, and she
locked her hands again and pulled like she could pop
his head clean off.

"I've got a message for Deacon Rice, Lefty." Polly
scooted him toward the open door, riding him like
an old-time Inch Worm toy. The blood from her thigh
soaked into his t-shirt. "This is who I'm sending for him.
Let Rice know you and your capitalistic pigs are going
down, you midget motherfucker."

But the vicious melee outside caught even Polly off
guard. The streetlights silhouetted two figures: One a
giant mass, the other a hummingbird – a hummingbird

that twirled a baseball bat like a bo and a broken cello like nunchucks. Jo delivered kicks and strikes so fast, the combinations blurred. It seemed the mountain of a man wanted to fall, but Jo was so damn quick, she kept him standing by knocking him back and forth – off balance to on balance. Each time the bat met its target, a loud thwack resounded, but each time, the thwack sounded wetter and wetter and wetter. When the midget tosser's knees appeared to give, Jo'd kick him in the dick, straightening him long enough to deliver another flurry of punishment.

Beneath Polly, Lefty Gonzales squirmed. His cries were those of an injured beast. When his partner finally dropped like a sack of vomit, Lefty's chest heaved with sobs, and Polly slid the slimy faux-dick from his mouth.

"Get his giant ass out of here before he stinks up the neighborhood."

From the beaten behemoth's bloody body, Jo turned her attention to the RV and pointed with the baseball bat. Between the yellowed backlighting from the streetlamp and the glittering, glass-crusted pavement, she could have been mistaken for a superhero, drawn in a perfect opening panel – a halo circling her. "You're next, motherfucker!"

"No," Polly said. "I need the little one. Let him be."

"I wasn't talking to him, bitch."

#

February 2013. Dreamland in the Dakotas:

Abigail wore her dance dress, the one with the purple and gold sequins arranged to resemble overalls and cut so short, her sagging, aged ass hung half out. She and Jo danced to the music with no volume, on a strobe-light-ed floor, existing in otherwise total blackness. Together alone. But Jo sensed they were not truly alone.

It was the version of Abigail from closer to the end – after they'd gotten to her. After they'd poisoned her and left her feeble and ill and too tired to be angry about it.

When she'd appear in the visions, she'd arrive in different versions of her living self. Jo was grateful for all of them. Jo was grateful to feel loved again. But this particular form of Abigail left Jo with a sense she needed to protect her dead wife.

Jo became aware of a presence lurking behind her. However, every time she tried turning to face whatever skulked about, the entire floor swiveled.

"Don't worry about it now," Abigail smelled faintly of cloves and smoke. "Can we just enjoy our time?"

"Worry?" And Jo realized she was worried, but couldn't pinpoint why. Couldn't single out one cause more important than the million others that should bother her. "I worry about nothing when I'm with you, Abs."

"You're so full of shit, your eyes have gone brown." Abigail twirled, fell back into Jo's arm and waited for a kiss.

The presence behind Jo seemed to draw closer. Oppressive. The dance floor whirled so rapidly as she turned her head trying to catch a glimpse, Jo couldn't orient herself and felt as if she was about to lose her balance. The dance floor dropped in freefall, the abyss around rushing past.

"Would you hurry up and kiss me, damnit! We don't have long."

"Why? What's coming, Abs?"

"A shit storm. Isn't that always what's coming?"

Jo grabbed the gray, hippy-style ponytail behind Abigail's head, pulled her close, and unleashed a long, sloppy one on the money maker. When she opened her eyes, Abigail was gone.

Polly'd taken up residence in Jo's arms. "I've missed you, you little bitch." The words were silent and Jo needed to read her lips. The dance floor had disappeared. The dark turned all white – a blanket of snow unfolding for miles. No horizon. No sky. Dirty and gloomy and foggy and hopeless.

"Where's Abigail?"

"Who gives a fuck?" Polly mouthed.

"I'm here, Jo," the environment said in Abigail's voice – her strong voice. An undercurrent of cello played background to the Abs' words, a strong aroma of cloves proliferated. "Get done what needs to get done. Do it and move past her. We'll be together soon enough."

Polly said something, but her lips didn't move. Jo could only tell because she felt it in her chest, a branding iron against her heart. Polly cackled like a stereotypical comic-book villain – the laugh drowning out Abigail's cello accompaniment. The laugh coming in waves, louder and louder.

Jo opened her eyes. She focused on the unfamiliar surroundings as she caught her bearings.

And she knew Abigail, like usual, had been right. The shit storm was full-on upon her.

# # #

October 2006. A Kansas cornfield, and Toto nowhere in sight:

Make no mistake: The shenanigans of the evening's entertainment held no sway over Jo Martindale. Not at first, anyway. She attended the night club and witnessed the festivities for business and business alone. She figured one week to complete the unpleasant task. One lousy, long week and she'd be gone, returned to her former life, maybe somehow worming her way back into Julliard, perhaps – preferably – with Polly in tow.

That's how little Jo Martindale knew about The Money Run. That's how little she knew about Polly Amorous.

Two days before, Polly, her sweet Polly, had dropped her on a lost Kentucky highway held together more by dead weeds than asphalt. "This is it – one of the few routes we know they still use," Polly had said between goodbye kisses. "I don't have any idea how long you'll have to wait out here, but you're on your own starting this second." She'd slid her hand under Jo's Tweety Bird sweatshirt, beneath her bra and grasped the iPhone held in place by the strap. "No cell phones. No way to trace you back to PAGANS."

"But I just bought that."

"I'll keep it for you. It's in good hands." She reached across and opened the passenger door. "But if they find out you're one of us, shit'll be a million times worse. You'll hope for a quick death." Polly began fiddling with the phone while talking.

"So – Empire State Building rooftop. Two weeks, right?"

"Just like the movies, you romantic bitch." She grabbed Jo by the pink bun, pulled her right and tight and kissed her with a vigorous violent might that Jo so loved.

"What if it takes longer? How do I find you?"

Polly half sighed/half laughed. It should have been a hint. "Follow the yellow-brick road." She pinched Jo on her crooked nose despite how often Jo had complained over the gesture. "I'll find you, Jo. I promise, I'll find you." With that, Polly presently pushed Jo out the passenger door. "Not to put any undue pressure on you, but future generations all over this world are depending on you. Kill the bastard and the get the fuck outta Dodge as fast as your bitch ass can." She blew a final kiss. "Love ya'."

Then, she was gone. In Jo's Prius, with Jo's phone, she disappeared over the horizon, and Jo found herself abandoned on the infamous Money Run – about to meet the love of her life and kill more malicious motherfuckers than she'd ever imagined one could without aid of a nuclear device. It didn't look likely at that particular moment, though.

Jo absorbed her surroundings, noting every detail to keep her grounded, and sort of expected Money Run goblins to emerge from the trees and have their wicked ways with her. She was mildly disappointed when nothing happened. "So...what in the hell do I do now?" Without a clear answer, she began walking in no direction in particular.

Miles and hours later, the fall sun threatening to drop, the breeze biting through her sweatshirt, not a single vehicle had found its way down the weed-choked road. Her backpack straps had rubbed her armpits raw, and Jo considered maybe she'd been had. It wasn't as if trust had served as a pillar in her and Polly's arrangement anyhow. It had no chance to considering the circumstances under which their relationship had begun.

Still, the idea of some underground matrix, a loose-knit network of back alleys and forgotten byways that served as the pipeline for ninety-nine percent of the illegal mumbo-jumbo going down in the good ol', red-white-and-blue, apple-pie-eating, US of the motherfucking A sounded plausible back in the Winnebago bed, naked and sweaty during the summer's hot nights, but now, forsaken in fucking Kentucky at dusk, in autumn, the thought felt inane. Fucking Money Run.

For the first time since she'd nearly killed the midget tosser in Maxville's RV park, tears formed. Jo's heart hammered like John Henry on a meth cocktail, while electric worms crawled between her layers of skin. Breaths came too fast for her to keep up. Thoughts passed without registering, one crashing into the next, all pointing toward panic.

The sobbing threatened to become a full-on episode. Recognizing this, as she always did, Jo sat – cross-legged – in the middle of the road with the crescent moon peaking over the tree-covered mountains to the east. She closed her eyes. Regulated her breathing. Pictured her palpitating heart, her tightening stomach, and crawled into herself. Into and aboard the runaway train of blood burrowing through the tunnels of her circulatory system. She envisioned herself applying the engine's brake and slowing the platelets to a manageable, orderly speed. Then her attention turned to slowing her heart. Soothing it so the muscle no longer beat frantically against her rib cage, trying to escape her body. Calming it. Letting it know everything would be okay. Breathing. Breathing. Always breathing.

She heard Dvorak's Cello Concerto Number Four all around her. She pictured the left-hand technique for the piece. Imagined performing it on Polly's swollen clitoris. She'd found her happy place. In that state, she swore she levitated – literally and figuratively.

Jo had no idea how long she'd been inside when she opened her eyes, but the sky had gone full dark, clouds hiding the heavens. Her ass sat firm on the cold asphalt. A semi-truck idled behind her. Its headlight beams pasted a hundred foot shadow of Jo on the road. The horn blared. From the cab, the unmistakable "Why Don't We Get Drunk?" chorus by Jimmy Buffet blared.

"Hell of a place for a sit-in," the driver yelled in slurred speech as he rolled down the window. "You're damn lucky I saw you at all."

In her new, serene state, Jo stood. "I guess I am. Any chance I get lucky enough for a lift?"

The driver wiped his face as if removing a spider web. "Like there's any other options. Hop your happy ass in."

And that driver, Jo's first interface with a Run inhabitant, and his pitchers of margaritas, Hawaiian print shirt and Jimmy Buffet jamming non-stop on the stereo had driven Jo to The Pit – a cinderblock building rising from a Kansas cornfield so far removed from civilization, no another light could be seen. That driver had promised she'd find at least an inkling of a hint of a beginning of a lead on Deacon Rice's whereabouts therein. During their travel, he'd offered no additional information on her target and had turned up the stereo every time she'd tried tilting the conversation that way.

At the conclusion of their drive together, he'd ducked inside The Pit long enough to refill two, one-gallon jars with margaritas and had wished her good luck. "And by good luck, I mean I hope you don't find what you're looking for. Or he doesn't find you first. I ain't got clue one what you're up to, Jo, but I know this much:

You, miss, are in way over your damned head. Just be discreet."

"I've made it this far, haven't I?"

The driver had scanned the barroom and had stolen a sip from one of the jars. "So'd all these morons. You take care of yourself, you hear?"

"I hear," she'd answered.

The Pit's jukebox played olden, crusty country songs. Not in Jo's wheelhouse, but a welcome reprieve from Margaritaville. Freddy Fender crooned – background music for the debauchery celebrated in every nook and corner of the barroom. The club reeked of stale beer and marijuana and sweat and sex and sin. Several people within the many gatherings openly prepared syringes with various concoctions. In a booth, some whore dressed in a nun's habit performed handjobs on two truckers, one on either side, while a third satisfied himself in the facing seat. With a straw, the hooker nun sucked down the pitcher of beer while executing her duties. At least a dozen empty shot glasses littered the table separating her from the masturbating voyeur.

So, Jo thought, this is motherfucking Kansas.

Amid the madness, the main event demanded center stage. An assemblage of deplorables surrounded what appeared to be a shortened bowling lane in the middle of the room. Cash – lots of it, as in movie prop amounts – passed casually from one bettor to the next, each participant looking like an extra from an apocalyptic biker movie, all obviously well lubricated.

The screech of feedback interrupted Freddy Fender, and a booming voice from some unseen god announced over the PA: "Welcome to the 2006 Dwarfapalooza National Champeeeenship!"

Applause erupted. Even patrons with needles protracting from their arms joined, syringes flapping about wildly. Other announcements emerged but unintelligible to Jo, and she wondered if she needed to be as inebriated as the collected clientele to decode them. Yet, cheers punctuated each pause. Jo couldn't pull her attention away despite having no hint to the nature of the goings on.

These distractions allowed Lefty Gonzales to sneak behind her and jam a pistol into the small of her back. "What's a skanky whore like you doing in a nice place like this?"

The dwarf had made a crucial mistake, though. Should Jo have chosen, she could've relieved him of his weapon and broken his tiny body in half simply because he'd allowed himself to get too close. However, Jo chose not to. Not yet, anyway.

"How's the knee little man? That sure looked grizzly last time I saw it."

"It's good enough to put a foot up your dyke ass." He nudged her with the pistol barrel. "Where's your chink friend?"

"She's not Chinese."

"Who gives a flying fuck?"

"I'm kind of particular about my racial epithets. Like, for a bite-sized Mexican, I'd go wi--"

The midget jammed the gun deeper into Jo's lower spine, probably because the upper spine would have been too great a reach. She responded by preparing a back kick aimed dead for his bad knee. Then, a drunken hippy in overalls and high heels fell on Lefty Gonzales, both tumbling to the sticky cement floor.

"Oh, I'm sorry, fine sir." The stranger got up and dusted off her knees before extending a hand to the midget. "I couldn't see you there. You're a wee one, ain't you?" Her expression told Jo she knew exactly what she'd done and somehow communicated it'd be in Jo's best interest to play along.

Lefty must have picked up on it, too. Instead of accepting the hippy's offer of assistance, he scrambled for the pistol he'd dropped in the collision. The woman's ruby-red sequined stiletto blocked him and its heel ground into the back of his hand.

"Damnit, Abigail, this ain't your concern." The midget's voice devolved into a high-pitched scream of pain.

"I'm making it my concern." She bent and picked up the gun, holding the barrel by two fingers as if it were a spent diaper. She handed the pistol to Jo, then helped Lefty up by his stump. "I know you have no qualms with this fine young lady, do you Lefty?"

Lefty didn't answer and wouldn't look at the hippy. He glowered at Jo instead. Chest heaving with deep, angry breaths, he snorted. His mullet had grown back in spots, some scarring still visible beneath the careful comb-over, but he seethed, just as pissed off as that night in May.

Abigail looked to Jo, as well. Ogled her. Appeared to have approved but spent a little too long looking at Jo's nose and its unusual angles. "This fellow have any qualms with you?"

"Possible qualms. More like misgivings. Me and Mighty Mouse here have a history, you might say."

"Really?" Her surprise appeared genuine. "Here I thought this a no-qualm zone. I hope Lefty's not violating that. Serious repercussions for a no-qualm zone infraction."

Jo laughed harder than she should have, and because of that, felt herself blush – something she'd rarely experienced.

"Abigail, you don't want to get bogged down in this." Lefty rubbed the back of his hand against his tank top as he stared at the gun Jo aimed at him. "This ain't a threat. It's a courtesy."

"I'd hate to call anybody a liar, Lefty, but you're not exactly known for adhering to the gentleman's code." The woman addressed the midget, but kept her gaze trained on Jo. Her long gray hair was pulled into a ponytail and her eyebrows had been plucked and redrawn into almost comical arcs. Her skin was aged but smooth, except for the crows' feet surrounding her eyes. She was thin and tall and graceful and a few stray gray hairs hung from her chin in a hapless array. Not classically beautiful in any way, but undeniably beautiful in her own way.

In the background, the PA god garbled to a particularly exuberant round of cheers. Vanilla Ice's "Ice Ice Baby" began its stolen bass line.

"They're calling you Lefty," the hippy said. "Wouldn't want to keep your adoring public waiting, would you?"

"Shit!" Lefty spat. He appeared to consider his options and spat again. "Steer clear of this one, Abigail." He pointed at Jo with his stump like he'd use it as a battering ram. "Deacon's got the cunt marked. That sick motherfucker's taken a personal interest in her."

"That makes two of us," Abigail said.

"What do you mean 'marked'?" Jo asked.

Another PA announcement, and the Vanilla Ice riff re-started. Lefty pivoted in a huff and carved his way through the crowd toward the center of The Pit. Soon, a path opened for him. Several onlookers patted his head or his back as he passed before closing the clearing behind him, swallowing the tiny man in a mass of depravity.

"What'd he mean, 'marked'?"

"I've always had a thing for Vanilla Ice," Abigail said. He kind of makes me question my inner lesbian."

"What? Wait – really?"

Abigail stood side-by-side with Jo, arms folded, each facing the crowd surrounding the bowling lane. The gathering exploded with cheers. Above their heads, the One-Armed Bandit corkscrewed through the pot-smoke haze tinted with neon beer-brand lights.

"Yeah, really – something about a white rapper, I guess. I don't know, just makes me tingly. Then I meet somebody like you and remember how good I am at this lesbian thing."

"I suppose you want me to take that as a compliment."

"It's meant as one." Abigail nudged Jo in the ribs with a playful elbow.

"I'm spoken for." Although Jo wondered how true that statement was. She'd been with Polly only two days before, but it felt much longer – almost like a past life that fell further away with each mile she'd traveled across America's underbelly.

"I ain't asking you to marry me darlin'. You haven't even bought me a drink yet."

Jo fought the smile tugging at her mouth.

"Hell, young lass with your pretty ass, we ain't even hit the sack, yet. Not going to buy any car without a test drive."

Jo again giggled more than the quip warranted. "Yet, huh?"

"Well, the night's still young."

Jo nestled the pistol in the back of her pants thinking she'd rather shoot her ass off than stick it in front and have a real issue. "What did he mean marked?"

"Depends. How'd you piss off Deacon Rice?"

"Never met the man. I assume it's a man." Feigning ignorance despite not knowing why she should.

The hippy touched Jo's chin, tipped her face so their gazes met. "Don't lie to me young lass. You have no idea how much shit you're in right now, and I'm the closest thing you got to a friend."

"Friend? You move pretty fast, huh?"

AC/DC's "Thunderstruck" boomed from The Pit's sound system, appropriately and riotously greeted by the heathens. More announcements. More cheers. Somebody busted a beer bottle on the cement floor, and others followed suit.

"Who are you?" Abigail said. "You got history with Lefty but I ain't never seen you before."

"You know all of Lefty's acquaintances."

"It's my business to know such things." She reached into the bib pocket of her overalls and removed a clove cigarette and a lighter. She handed the lighter to Jo. "Fact is, you don't know who I am, do you?"

Jo flicked the lighter and held the flame to the cigarette. "Should I?" She already knew the answer, though. The first pounds of the enormity of her task began weighing on her.

"Fact number two: That response means you definitely need a friend." Abigail blew the stinky sweet smoke from the corner of her mouth. She held the cigarette cocked in her arm, ever at the ready for another drag. "You've already pissed off some people – Deacon Rice knows who you are, but you couldn't find your ass with two hands and a flashlight. Shit don't add up."

"I can take care of myself."

"Right – you fucking let Lefty get the drop on you." She inhaled another drag. "Speaking of which, you're going to want to exit stage left pretty soon here. Bandit's not the type to just let things slide. Some Napoleonic Complex shit going on with that little psycho."

Jo lost the tug-of-war with her smile. Abigail flashed hers, as well, but the nice moment turned awkward for Jo. She wish she'd offered some pithy comeback, but thought of none.

"I let him think he had the drop on me." Jo wanted to turn away, maybe pretend to watch the midget tossing, but some force kept her focused on Abigail. With the whirl of activity in The Pit, the hippy oozed a sense of calm and comfort.

"You going to make it in this world, you need to quit deluding your young self. How long you been in it?"

"It?"

"The Run." Abigail inhaled another drag, this time blowing the plum full on in Jo's face followed by a full-throttled smile. "You're a cute miss thing – except for that nose – but if you don't start coming clean with me, I'll leave you to these wolves, understand? You're fresh meat and not a one of these motherfuckers would say 'boo,' 'poo,' or 'coo-coo-cachoo' you turn up dead." She took a step closer, and Jo smelled the day's work on the other woman. "Or you end up worse."

"I said I can handle my fucking self."

"Really? Then what's Deacon Rice want with you?"

"Maybe you should be asking what I want with Deacon Rice." Jo snatched the clove cigarette from Abigail just to demonstrate she could. "Because I'm here to kill him real good." She tossed the cigarette to the sticky floor because she didn't know what else to do, and wondered why she was trying so hard to impress the older woman. Subconsciously, she knew, though.

Abigail's smile turned into a smirk. "Kill Rice?" She took the lighter back from Jo and lit another clove cigarette. "Think I know who this girlfriend of yours is now. If I'm right, you're gonna need a hell of a lot more than a friend."

In the background, P!nk's "Get the Party Started" blasted. The PA announced another competitor. More of The Pit's revelers amassed around the center of the bar, several standing on tables. Newly emptied bottles smashed. In the chaos, a passing mountain of a drunkard pinched Jo's ass.

So, it was on.

Jo spun and caught the fat fuck beneath the ribs with her elbow, the crack audible over the surrounding commotion. As he bent from the blow, Jo whirled, rolled over his back and slipped her forearm under his neck, riding him like a drugged bull. With her other arm, she grabbed the back of his head and created an arm bar, her forearm across his larynx.

"From right here, I could kill this piece of shit six different ways using my bare hands."

Abigail answered with a slow clap. None of the other patrons seemed to notice.

"Still think I can't take care of myself?"

Instead of answering, Abigail reached into her bib pocket again, this time producing a Chinese star she held between her first two fingers. With a wrist flick, she flung the projectile. It whistled past Jo's knee close enough for her to feel the breeze.

Behind her, Lefty Gonzales screeched. The star had caught him in the back of his hand and he dropped a pen knife. He had been within striking distance of Jo.

"I think you could probably use some adult supervision, still," Abigail said. "Just a thought."

# # #

May 2006. Last shift in Maxville:

Mr. Gurley, the counter manager, had allowed Jo to clock out early before the dinner rush. He offered no thanks. Said no goodbyes. Ignored the elephant in the room, reminded her to take her wrestling trophy, and disappeared into the kitchen as Jo took leave for the final time. The counter had been dead anyway, as if townsfolk had avoided it all day. Even the streets on the ride home appeared more deserted. In her mind, the moment should have been heavier. Like the route lined with everybody who'd wronged her in this shitty little town, all eager to apologize and begging her to stay. She'd earned a parade allowing a final "fuck you" directed at each of the fucks she shouldn't give a fucking fuck about. All the past prom queens and wanna-be prom queens crying and pregnant with fetal rednecks who'd grow up to think Maxville and its barn dances and harvest festivals was all life had to offer. Their infernal offspring would, in turn, knock up future prom queens and future wanna-be prom queens until the town was so inbred, children with third eyes and single digit IQs would be the norm. That time wasn't far off, Jo thought.

Still, she hoped against hope when she turned down Black Gully Lane, her parents' F150 would be parked in its usual spot out front of the house. She ignored the pang of pain, the tiny nip at her ego, when the space sat unoccupied. She pulled into it and cut the Prius' engine.

The CD player continued Ravel's "Bolero," and Jo strained her trained ears, focused, allowing herself to swim in the strings. She listened to the entire piece and daydreamed of performing it, starring front and center with an acclaimed orchestra. When it was over, she opened the car door, thinking the first step to accomplishing that dream would be to pack.

After grabbing the mail which included the usual couple of pieces from Julliard, Jo strode across the asphalt drive toward the back garage where she'd lived – by mutual arrangement with the parents – since sophomore year at Maxville High. Next door, a familiar 2006 Mustang pulled into the drive. Jo hastened her pace, but couldn't escape.

"Hey, Lezzy Jo. How you doing?" Sandy Gurley exited the Mustang. She wore an oversized Iowa State sweatshirt, too-tight shorts thanks to the freshman fifteen, and a tan deeper than it should be considering the time of year. Years earlier, Sandy had outted Jo to half the middle school, although she'd conveniently omitted the parts in which Sandy herself had partaken.

"What are you doing home?" Jo asked.

"Finals are next week. Already decided I ain't going back, so no sense in sticking around." Sandy popped the trunk and pulled out two duffle bags. "You going to be around later? Maybe we can catch up." She held up one of the bags to draw Jo's attention to it. "I got some wine coolers."

The possibility of accepting crossed Jo's mind. Sandy, per their history, only wanted to drink with Jo for one reason. It would serve as a fitting farewell to the Maxville era for Jo to be the one leaving this time. Then, for no reason she could discern, an image of that Polly lady flashed through Jo's thoughts. "Maybe a little later. If I'm not too busy."

"Sure thing. You check that packed social calendar and let me know."

Jo caught the dull end of the verbal knife's little twist. Right there, she decided against revenge sex in favor of expediting her exit from the hostile home town that existed wholly to hate her. That decision, the power to leave, inspired a feeling of freedom. It elated her, and under the spell of this new euphoria, she opened the side door to the garage, ready to put her past where it belonged.

Until the present sucker-punched her in the gut.

Inside, silver spray paint desecrated the back cinderblock wall, spelling out "DYKE" in four-foot tall letters. Dozens of Bruce Lee, Cynthia Rothrock and Jackie Chan posters, torn and fresh with water damage, littered the concrete floor, and her Everlast heavy bag, already held together by duct tape, had been sliced open, top-to-bottom and dissected, the filling, wet and yellow, mixed in with the poster remnants. Her collection of kung-fu DVDs, shattered, lay strewn across her unmade bed.

Jo knew she should be enraged. Understood whomever pulled this wanted to scare her and make her feel ugly. Instead, numbness filled her. Confusion. Why, on all possible days, would anybody mess with her then? She was as good as fucking gone, and nobody wanted her to stay. Nobody. She began to catalogue possible perpetrators when her inner alarm went off.

Where was Beatrice?"

In the sparsely furnished room – her bed, a dresser, a practice stool, a TV stand comprised of more cinder blocks and plywood – the absence of her cello should have been the first thing she'd have noticed. Her heart sank, threatened to escape into her churning stomach, when she espied the tuning peg box sticking out from under her bed. Jo crept to the twin-size, knowing she didn't want to see whatever laid in wait on the other side.

There, she found her opened case. Beatrice's body rested inside shattered into a thousand cheerless pieces. The red faux-velvet lining looked like blood flowing among the wooden shards and splinters. Jo screamed with an agony that caused her throat to bleed. And screamed. And screamed.

She stumbled through the rubble to the small bathroom. Gagging echoed in the enclosed space, and doubled in volume as wave after wave of vomit evacuated Jo's body. After she thought there was no more to give, she threw up again, stomach acid scorching her esophagus and the taste of the bile pervading her mouth. With her work uniform apron, she wiped away the remnants from her chin and the snot covering her upper lip. Her back found the wall, and she slid slowly down until her butt met the floor. She hugged her knees. Rocked slightly. Cried – for a very long time. Until the room was as dark as her mood.

The whole of her world existed simply in that small space in that tiny bathroom, utterly and totally alone.

A good time later, once she'd exhausted her supply of tears, she focused her breath and began the trance – went inside, as she'd come to call it after years of practice. Jo listened to the darkness and noted every detail possible about the violent vandalism of her personal space. Explored her mind and every emotion, picking at them – bathing in them. She wanted to remember the turmoil of that evening. The feelings of helplessness and anger and alienation that had inundated her. She needed to burn the reason she'd never return to Iowa into her brain in case, for some unknown ludicrous reason, she'd ever suffer a bout of homesickness. For a good hour or so, Jo memorized everything and how everything felt.

Because she was going to make some motherfucker pay someday.

She returned from her meditative state and stood on shaky, cramping legs, taking a moment to ensure she could go on. Through the darkness, she felt her way through the garage's side door and made her way to the darker main house. She entered through the unlocked back door because no need existed for locked doors in Maxville. So long as you fit in, Jo thought.

Inside, she turned on the light to reveal the loneliness that saturated the Victorian farm house. The tick-tock of the antique coo-coo clock seemed louder than it should have been, a bomb timer counting toward detonation. Two chairs, and only two chairs, accompanied the kitchen table. Picture frames over the fireplace mantle had been replaced with Beanie Babies posed in positions supposed to be adorable, but turned out kind of suggestive.

Jo headed straight for that same living room fireplace, dislodged the loose bricks at the back and found her father's moonshine jug – only a quarter full, but it'd do the trick. She popped the cork and drew in a gulp that barreled through her like a flamethrower the entire way down. After a belch that'd embarrass a frat pledge, she inhaled a longer drink. The numbness was immediate. Isolation – being alone in such a large house while alone in such a small town – loomed heavy, an overwhelming blanket of dour emotion that might well paralyze her, and Jo wanted to run away for a safe place, but she had none anymore. Not with the violation of her garage.

As she considered this, she found herself, no-so-co-incidentally, outside her former bedroom. Or as her mother often put it, the new sewing space/yoga studio. Since the church elders met with Jo's parents four years before, and the family decided Jo moving outside would be best for all involved, Jo hadn't entered that room – for that matter, had been in the house only for holidays. According to her mother, the bedroom had been repurposed before that weekend had ended. Jo's entire childhood erased in a two-day span. The door permanently closed to her. The urge to inflict that room with the same treatment her garage received swelled within Jo's veins.

Another swig off the jug provided the courage to open the door. The fury inside her provided the impetus.

In the room, though, instead of a sewing machine, she found her old queen-sized bed – freshly made and draped with her Toy Story II comforter. Where she pictured yoga mats would've taken root, her white dresser stood. The photos of her and her family at different karate tournaments remained situated exactly as she'd left them, nary a speck of dust sullying their mismatched frames. Dress patterns or downward dog posters didn't cover the wall, rather her old cello competition ribbons still hung, medals freshly polished. Over her vanity table, the oval mirror hadn't been tampered with either – still shattered in innumerable pieces. Each shard displayed the image of Jo, eyes brimming with tears around her crooked nose and pink hair a matted mess, looking into them.

As she stared, the images melted, then transformed, and she saw the younger Jo in those reflections. One shard showed her getting her first black belt and the pride her parents shared as they hugged her tight enough to crush ribs. Another replayed one of her zillions of cello recitals, Mom and Dad front and center, beaming, making sure the audience members knew it was their daughter, the Martindale girl, who'd just wowed everyone. In yet another, she rode bikes with Sandy Gurley and the neighborhood kids, carefree and intoxicated by friendships that'd surely last a lifetime. In each piece of the mirror, she saw visions that made her feel she'd belonged in Maxville. Sure, she was different and always knew it, but the mirror reminded her of times when it didn't seem to matter.

Until one day it did.

And everybody could relax because Jo was the one – the outcast who people pointed out and gossiped about and thanked their ever-loving righteous god that their child wasn't like that.

Jo sat on the bed as if the memories anchored her there. The mail in her back pocket crinkled under her weight. Deciding the need for an emotional pick-me-up, she pulled out the envelopes and opened the first from Julliard.

That's when her day really went to shit.

#

February 2013. The Dakota love shed:

Jo awoke to kisses – violent, feverish, I-will-kiss-you-and-you-will-like-it kisses. She would've pushed Polly – her not-sweet-at-all Polly – away, but her hands had been bound behind the chair in which she sat. To escape the barrage, she twisted her head, but Polly found her lips time after time.

"Jesus Christ! Stop it already. What are you – a puppy?"

"I'd go more with a kitty, but it's your analogy," was what Jo thought Polly said, but the words were difficult to make out as her vision was still a little blurry – her mind a little foggy. One eye had swollen mostly shut, from Polly's elbow or the car's cartwheels, Jo didn't know. Polly straddled Jo's lap and planted several more persistent pecks. She'd stripped Jo to her panties

– granny style as that's what Abigail had preferred – and the breast plate, which would've taken an instruction manual and a team of Army engineers to remove for anybody unfamiliar with it.

"Untie me."

"That doesn't sound like the Jo I know."

Jo arched her back, bucked, and tipped the chair. Polly slid off Jo's bare, sweaty thighs onto the stained area rug covering most of the frozen dirt floor. Foul light from the sole hanging bulb lit the room, but left shadows and their possible malevolent inhabitants everywhere. On the far wall, the ancient potbelly stove straight out of an old-timey western blasted full tilt. The heat permeated the shed. It turned the small dwelling into a large oven, and sweat poured from Jo. The stove singed the faint hair off her calf. She half worried some of her enhanced parts might melt. She full worried the heat might ignite the breastplate's propane.

With her foot, she pinned Polly to the rug and leaned the chair forward to utilize all her weight. "We both know you're going to unbind me sooner or later." Towering over her former lover infused Jo with a sense of dominance that wove itself into the usual adrenaline rush from doing her job. Her body tingled and goose pimples dotted her skin despite the oppressive heat. "Undo me now before you put me in a seriously bad mood."

Polly grabbed the naked foot planted on her drenched white camisole and inched it up her chest as she writhed. "We both know a lot of fucking things, don't we, Josephine?" She extended her tongue and lapped at Jo's big toe.

"Let me fucking go!" Jo maneuvered her foot beneath Polly's chin and pressed lightly on her throat, jabbing just enough to let her ex know she could still kill her in innumerable awful ways. Truly painful ways. "I don't like being tied up."

"Since when?"

"Since Deacon fucking Rice!" Jo applied pressure with her foot. Visions of the last time she'd been bound to a chair percolated. Her mind played that song he sang, the last thing she'd ever hear. It was all she could do to not snap Polly's larynx right then. Had it been anybody else, she likely would have.

"Yet you're here because of him, right? The deacon sent you." Polly's face flushed a painful shade of red and her mouth contorted in such strange shapes, it was a challenge to read her lips. "This isn't you just checking in to say 'hey,' right? Stopping by for a quickie? I didn't think so."

"You've really pissed him off this time. Typical Polly charm at work, I guess."

"Worked on your eyes, didn't it?" Jo thought Polly said before realizing the correct word was "ass." Polly snipped for Jo's ankle, but caught only hot air. "If I untie you, you're going to kill me. You said it your fucking self." She attempted another nip at the ankles like some incensed, meth-fueled Chihuahua. "I don't believe you, but that's what you said."

"Let me go or not – I'm killing you either way. Should do it just for the principle. You owe me a lot of money, Polly."

"Then your bitch eyes (correction – ass) might as well die with me out here. Together at last." Her grin, while indubitably attempting to be smug, strained her face and she looked like she was about to dump a hundred-pound shit. "That door." She nodded. "That one that's the only way out – I have it cooked up with enough C4 to keep a horde of map drawers busy for a long damn time. Either we're both leaving this mother-fucker here, or we're both dying here."

"Polly, you never disappoint in disappointing me." Jo cocked her wrist, releasing a micro spring attached to the tendon, a feature added during one of her dozens of cosmetic-slash-armament surgeries – Doc Edsel specials as Abigail had called them. A half-foot-long blade erupted from the forearm just beneath the Yo Ma-Ma tattoo. Another flick of the wrist, and she was free from the chair and zip tie. She raised the blade, threatening Polly. "I gave you a chance to be nice. Remember that."

Before Jo could strike, or even decide if she wanted to, Polly slipped her hand under the grimy rug and revealed a familiar two-headed dildo. She whipped it against Jo's knee. The momentary shift in momentum allowed her to roll from under Jo and scramble for the corner by the stove where she gained her feet. "How could you, Jo? How could you betray me and work for that evil son-of-a-bitch."

"I betrayed you?" Jo flicked her wrist again, and the blade re-sheathed, disappearing into the special forearm pouch. "I busted my ever-loving ass to get to the Empire State Building. I waited all damn day for you. Nearly froze my ass off."

"Aww...just like the movie."

"But you're no movie star." Jo adopted a fighting stance, determined to keep Polly pinned in the corner while mulling possibilities of disarming the door. Seeing Polly in the soaked spaghetti-string camisole, nipples armed and ready, kept distracting her, though, and she wondered for the millionth time if it was racist to prefer Asian women. Decided for the millionth time it probably was, but didn't care. "You were just being a cunt, weren't you? You never planned on being there. Not from day fucking one."

"You didn't exactly keep your end of the bargain either, Miss High-and-fucking-mighty. Deacon Rice is still on the wrong side of the sod." Polly rubbed the blood back into her neck and kept the enormous dildo pointed at Jo as if it were an actual threat – a weapon of mass orgasm. "What do you owe him, Jo? That cocksucker took your hearing."

"Maybe, but what do I owe you. Huh, Polly? Because you took my fucking soul."

"Like you have one."

"You stole my future."

"Get pissed off all you like, Josephine, but this is the life you were meant to have. You know it. I know it – knew it the first day I met you. You took to it like a junky to smack. You're just on the wrong fucking team now."

"I'm on my own side now."

"Like I said – wrong fucking team."

The heat battered Jo in mini waves that worked their way into her lungs and sapped at her energy. Sweat trickled into her good eye. Thoughts refused to relate to one another – one working on how to escape the rigged door followed by one of sharing that dildo with Polly followed by one of the grizzly task of decapitating her former lover for Deacon Rice's trophy case followed by one remembering Abigail and how just being in the same cramped confines with Polly equated to a certain level of infidelity. She wiped the sweat from her eye with her shoulder.

"What are we doing here, Jo?" Polly stepped forward into the full light and put on her best come-hither face. It would have been funny if it weren't so effective. "I got you. Right now, locked in here, I got you."

"You'd like to think so."

"I fucking know so."

Jo knew so, too. Half naked in the sweltering shed, alone with her first love, jacked with adrenaline. She knew this was inevitable from the minute Deacon Rice sent her out. Knew she somehow hoped for this part. Only this part.

"You don't want to kill me," Polly said.

"I've kind of wanted to kill you for a long damn time now."

"Only kind of?" Polly slung the sex toy over her shoulder and stepped even closer. Now, more in the light, her nipples were fully visible. Entirely fantastic.

"Well, I have my sentimental side, you know." Jo moved forward, as well.

"That's the Josephine, I know."

"Don't call me that!"

"Sorry. Jo." Polly reached to caress Jo's cheek. It might have been sweet if Jo had any nerves left in her face to feel the gesture. "My sweet Jo Martindale who wouldn't even change her name. The sentimental assassin."

"All this honeyed bullshit won't save you."

"I think it might. You know me, Jo." Polly slid her hand behind Jo's neck and pulled in for a soft kiss. "I've got plans to get us both out of this."

Jo placed her hands on Polly's hips and reeled her in. "Plans?"

# # #

Here was where the gratuitous, sweaty lesbian love scene took place. And it was spectacular.

#

"Still going to kill me?"

"You bet your sweet ass."

"Another go, then?"

"You bet your sweet ass."

#

March 2008. A faithful ride in the Maryland countryside:

Let it be known to all, with confusion for none: Jo Martindale had no intention of falling for Abigail nor the Money Run. The people from her past, Maxville folk, never hinted somewhere might exist where their little Lezzy Jo might not only fit in, she might flourish. A place she'd find respites of happiness, where she could be contented, even admired. Yet, while sitting in the passenger seat of Abigail's Mack diesel, listening to Sabbath's "War Pigs" on low volume, considering her next step after wrapping up the commitment they were en route to, Jo thought she might've stumbled into true love. Not fuck-me-fuck-me-now love, although that was a component, but an emotionally satisfying, spiritually fulfilling, mutual-respect love.

What that meant, she had not an iota of an idea. Oddly, she noted, she was more apprehensive facing such a notion than the task soon to be at hand.

"You better buck up, Buttercup," Abigail said. "This SOB isn't known for playing around."

"This bitch don't play, either."

"Oh, I keep forgetting. You're hardcore."

"Fucking A."

"Jesus. Tone it down. For me, at least."

"Sorry, Abs. Need to use that language. I'm a hard-core bitch."

"Keep telling yourself that, young lass."

"Somebody has to. You sure as shit don't believe it."

"Seriously? Every sentence?"

"Fucking A." Jo blew the dislodged soot from the Colt .45 barrel and spun the empty cylinder.

"Hardcore."

"As a bitch."

"Won't let me get the last word in, huh?"

"Fuck fucking no."

"Cuz you're a fucking assassin."

Before Jo could reply with the "Fucking A" she had loaded in the banter chamber, Abigail turned up Tony Iommi's solo and drowned her out. Jo would have thrown a dirty look, but couldn't stop the smile from her face.

Sun rays poured through the windshield, and the direct light warmed her. She turned down the stereo and slid off the University of Miami sweatshirt – a replica of the one Ice wore in the "Ice Ice Baby" video – but still felt overheated wearing only the t-shirt she had on underneath. "Funny how it can be so damn cold outside and so hot in here."

"Like we're ants and the windshield is a big old magnifying glass, and God's messing with us, seeing which shrivels first." There was no joking Abigail's voice. "Seeing if the other one will continue on the road to imminent doom."

"Know what I love most about you, Abs? Your supportive nature."

"Thanks." Abigail turned on the windshield juice to wipe away the collected bugs and dust. "I'm into your innocence – makes me feel like you need me."

"Ain't that fucking innocent." Jo licked her finger-tips, playful like. "That's what you're into."

"Fine then. You're naiveté. Like how you still think you're going to walk away from this unscathed." Abigail blew a plume of clove cigarette smoke from the corner of her mouth. The cigarette hung from the other cor-ner, bouncing with every rut in the road. "Even if you succeed, it won't amount to a pixel of difference in the big pic."

"Won't it? You've got to admit he's an evil motherfu--"

"You shut your mouth."

"Just talking about the deacon."

"Just tired of your constant profanity."

The semi's speedometer read one-fifteen. The Cadillac they pursued down the dirt county road wove to and fro, kicking up the largest possible dust cloud. Any hope of the Caddy's escape, though, hinged on ei-ther the Mack running out of fuel – chances of which were nil as she'd been topped off, reserve tanks and all, outside of Towson – or Abigail crashing. Since Abs drove better backwards, blindfolded and blitzed than the most skilled truckers sober, sighted and straight, the chance of the latter was as ludicrous as the former. From the passenger side of Lefty's car, a beer bottle ejected. Abigail swerved so smoothly, Jo needn't stop cleaning her revolver.

Around twenty minutes earlier, the Cadillac's occu-pants had stopped shooting at them. Jo'd figured they'd expended their ammo. She also figured that Abigail could put an end to this insipid chase any time she pleased. However, Abigail didn't please and didn't want this chase to end. Most likely she was still concocting ways to talk Jo out of going after Deacon Rice.

Once they had Lefty in tow, he'd set up a meeting. The One-Armed Bandit might need a little convincing to assist, but Jo kind of looked forward to changing his mind – another little demonstration for Abigail as to how hardcore she'd become in her scant months along The Run.

Jo clicked the cylinder back and forth several times, knocking free any loose debris onto the towel on her lap. The barrel reattached with a loud, satisfying snap, and she inserted the final pin. "Hardcore."

"Listen, Jo. I've been thinking..."

"Abs, even if I agreed with you, I'd still have to do this. You fighting it so damn hard just amps me up more."

"Then let me say my peace, already. What good is taking Deacon Rice out going to do? He's a sick puppy, yeah. But we know what we got with him."

Jo loaded the final round in the cylinder. "Not following you here."

"Nature abhors a vacuum – you're familiar with the idea, right?"

"Don't talk to me like I'm stupid. That drives me bat shit."

"All I'm saying is somebody else will fill Deacon Rice's smarmy-ass white loafers. You think killing him is going to kill the need for him? Motherfuckers want what motherfuckers want." Abigail placed her cigarette in the groove she'd drilled into the dash, hacked a few fierce phlegmy coughs, and spat the accumulated conglomeration into an empty coffee cup. She returned the cigarette back to her mouth, sucked on it like she truly loved it. Stinky sweet smoke drifted into her eye and she closed it until the wisp dissipated. "Greedy people ain't going anywhere. Lazy bastards ain't going to up and find a job or not cut corners. The need for The Run is still going to exist. Who's to say the next guy isn't worse than Rice?"

"This isn't some great moral crusade, Abs. It's not political – it's logical. If I don't get him, that motherfucker's going to get me. He knows I'm alive. He knows about me and Polly. That isn't some shit he'll let skate, because he don't let shit skate." Jo spun the cylinder, clicked it back into place and aimed the Colt at the Caddy. "He exposed Lefty to citizens – what do call them? The Heat? – just because he wanted take out Polly's Asian ass. What do you think he'll do to me? There's no running from him."

"But..."

"And if he knows about me, then he knows about you and me. How long you think you're going to keep getting plumb hauls? How long before he decides you need to go, too. What kind of example would he make of you?"

"I'm kind of a big deal, young lass. He won't get rid of me." Jo couldn't tell if Abigail winked or was simply blinking more smoke from her eye.

"If somebody can replace him, somebody would replace your wrinkly ass, too."

Abigail shook her head as if that would let her unhear the truth. "You're kind of hurting my feelings."

"If there's a Deacon Rice, there's no real future for you and me." Jo put her hand over Abigail's on the gearshift. "Sooner or later, that fake-nosed motherfucker is coming for us."

The driver shook her head harder, and Jo could almost see the thoughts forming through the imaginary smoke that should have been spewing from her ears, the realization evident in Abigail's eyes.

"Fuckity fuck fuck!" Abigail downshifted and punched the gas. Through the dust cloud, the Cadillac's brake lights glowed like devil-eyes special effects in some low-budget horror movie. The speedometer reached one-twenty-five. "For you, young lass."

"I love you." Jo's words hung in the dust-choked air like a lingering fart.

"What?"

Before Jo could respond, the semi tapped the Caddy's bumper. Abigail applied the brakes, and the duo witnessed the sedan drift sideways. Gravel pelted the Mack's windshield, and the dust plume mushroomed toward the sky, overtaking Jo and Abigail like an oncoming thunderstorm. Abigail swerved again as a tire hurled towards the semi's cab. Due to the speed it'd been travelling, the car slid for several dozen yards before coming to a complete stop. Once there, it teetered, two of the remaining wheels lifting from the ground, and threatened to roll before crashing back to the earth with a resounding and conclusive thud.

Jo exited the Mack before Abigail could say anything, anxious to get past her proclamation and get down to the business she so enjoyed. She aimed the revolver, Lefty's piece from their encounter at The Pit. The cold immediately struck her, and she half-thought of returning for her sweatshirt before deciding she was too hardcore for that shit. "You dead, Lefty?"

Another beer bottle whizzed past her head. The wind wake it left blew Jo's blue hair out of her face.

"Get your one-armed ass out here." Her aim started shaking as she couldn't control herself against the shivers. "And bring your boyfriend with you."

Abigail got down from the truck and wrapped an afghan she'd crocheted around Jo's shoulders. "Right back at you, young lass." She kissed Jo lightly on the cheek. "Right back at you." Abigail wouldn't again approach verbalizing her feelings for Jo in their five plus years together. For Jo, that would be enough, so long as she showed her every day.

"Jesus Christ, Abigail" Lefty said. "What'd you do that for?"

"Cuz I'm hardcore," Abigail answered.

Jo shot Abigail a scornful glance, but was laughing on the inside.

"Hardcore enough that you bitches are going to pay for this." Lefty limped around the car inspecting all the damage. "And the tow, too."

"Why you running from us?" Jo asked.

Lefty stomped forward with a pronounced limp. It would have been comical if he hadn't been so livid. Perhaps, actually probably, his agitation added to the abundant humor of his actions. "Cuz every time I see your bitch ass, I end up with stitches." He held up his hand to display the scar from Abigail's Chinese star. "Seems good enough reason to me. Better question is why you crazy wenches chasing us?"

"To hold you to your promise," Jo said.

"You playing games with me, bitch? You wrecked my car to fuck around?" He made his familiar angry face, crinkling his brow so the swastika sank away in the wrinkles. With the dust caught in his thin mustache, it gave an appearance of smoke blooming from his nostrils – a cartoonish, half-pint bull preparing to charge.

For a second, Jo thought she might actually have to fight him. For a second, she smiled. "You promised you were going to take me to see the Deacon."

Lefty's angry expression faded, he straightened and leaned back. Bewilderment clouded his eyes. "What?" He pointed at Jo, but looked at Abigail. "What the fuck is she talking about? You ran me down to see Rice? Why didn't you take her?"

"Come now, Lefty. Let's not deflect," Abigail said, her voice stern. "We need you to set up a meeting. I wouldn't chase you down if I didn't have a good reason, would I?"

The confusion on the midget's face appeared genuine.

"Don't waste our time," Jo said, her teeth chattering. "Take me to him."

"Why? What the fuck you dykes up to?"

"I'm gonna kill the motherfucker."

For a moment, Lefty stopped moving altogether, letting the idea sink in. The more he ruminated, it appeared, the more difficult it proved for him to grasp the idea. The hacking guffaw that exploded from the tiny man was most definitely genuine. He placed his hand and stump over the belly jiggling beneath the dirty down vest, and puffs of foggy breath chugged from him like a locomotive's smoke stack. "That's your plan, huh?"

"Don't like to complicate things." Jo tried maintaining some aura of menace, but the afghan covering her shoulders and the shivering barely allowed her a sense of dignity much less a projection of intimidation.

"Tell you what: I won't even charge a fee for this." Lefty looked to Abigail. He was saying more than his words expressed, but Jo couldn't pick up what unspoken messages had passed along. "I just get first crack when he turns her out. Sound fair, Abigail?"

"Fuck you."

"Hardcore, dear," Jo said

"Fuck you, too. Lefty's right. You don't pull this off, he's going to turn you into one of those sex zombies."

"Will you give me some fucking credit?"

"You going to throw your girlfriend to the wolves like this, Abigail?" Lefty asked.

Abigail rubbed her forehead as if fending off a headache. Her ponytail fluttered in the freezing breeze. "No talking any sense in this one."

"Ah, I see. If you love something, set it free kind of deal."

"Something like that."

Lefty rubbed his palm over his stump like an evil cartoon genius, before blowing into his hand and clasping it several times to warm up. "We have a deal, Ms. Hardcore?" he asked Jo.

"Not quite."

"Then forget it. I'm sure Abigail can find another way to help you fulfill your death wish."

"I'll agree to your terms, but what do I get when I prove you wrong?"

This time, the One-Armed Bandit doubled over, full-throttled midget guffaws wracking his itty-bitty body. "You name it, Jo. You name it."

"Then I believe we have a deal."

The bandit stopped laughing.

# # #

November 2007. Waiting on fate at a Jersey rest stop:

Abigail Freitag sucked on a clove cigarette, checked her watch again and cursed under her breath. Her tractor unit idled, the Mack's engine purring like a contented lion. The familiar rumble kept her from full on stir crazy, but not without a great effort.

The far end of the lot, the south part closest to the off-ramp, remained well-lighted. Abigail stayed on the north end, where the lights had been shot out so clandestine activity rest stops were so infamous for could be executed with little obstruction. This was as close as she'd allow herself to be exposed – to be "on the grid" – and not operating under the cover of The Money Run. And she realized, she wouldn't have done it for anybody else but Jo. Also realized she hated herself somewhat for that.

So the little shit, even with her tight ass and banging body, should think better of standing anybody up or Abigail would compound some of those angles in Jo's nose at their next encounter. If there were to be a next encounter.

A new set of headlights breached the north hill. As the car neared, the engine sound overcame the clamor from the turnpike. As with all the vehicles before, Abigail's hopes rose along with her heart rate. The sedan maneuvered its way further north than most of the other cars. She couldn't tell if it was a taxi, and the shadows didn't let her see if it contained more than one occupant. Abigail caught herself holding her breath.

Then, the car slowed. It parked. It wasn't a taxi. Again, it wasn't Jo. Abigail extinguished her butt, looked at her watch, and retrieved another clove cigarette from her overalls.

As carload after carload disappointed her, her hopes sank further, but the heart rate continued its upward climb. She wished she could pull Jo's Jedi meditation mumbo-jumbo to calm herself, but thinking about Jo made things worse. What if she wasn't coming back? What if Polly had talked her out of it? How long was Abigail to wait? At what point did it go from valiant and romantic and fulfilling her duty to pathetic?

Just as she reached that point when, by any standard, pathetic had become apparent, another car entered the rest area. A white limo Abigail recognized the moment it came into view, before the blaring "Only in America" by Brooks and Dunn thundered through the parking lot. Abigail flashed her headlights. The limo sped up, headed toward her, and parked so the driver side faced her. The tinted window rolled down.

The deacon was but a shadow, save for the prosthetic nose that refracted the light from the other side of the lot. Jo waited for him to cut the music before she lowered her window in turn.

Deacon Rice leaned out enough for his perfect salt-and-pepper pompadour to pop into view. "Polly never showed. Ash was there, ready to throw her over the fences, but she never showed." His measured, smooth, monotone voice creeped the fuck out of Abigail. "Your girl was still there when we left. She was crying."

Abigail blew a lungful of clove smoke at the limo. "Nah, she's too hardcore for that."

Deacon Rice gawked for a moment, appeared to gage Abigail's mood, before they both decided it was okay to laugh. When the awkwardness set in, the deacon continued. "What's your assessment?"

"She's bad-ass. She'll serve your purpose."

"Which one?"

"Well, she ain't doing squat to Polly. Not without that voodoo you do. She still has feelings for her." A small part of Abigail hurt to vocalize that particular truth. "That crazy terrorist must have a golden tongue or something."

"Don't sound so wistful."

Abs inhaled off her cigarette and tapped the steering wheel. "Does make me wonder why Polly has such a hold over her."

"I'm more curious as to what sway you have."

"You're golden. Don't fret. She's deadly and learns fast. She's a good kid."

Deacon Rice leaned further out the car window. "Kind of curious what sway she has over you."

"I'm all business, Deacon. You know that."

"Banging her still, right?"

"Every goddamned day. Anything for the job."

"Company girl always."

"That's me."

"Bullshit. Don't mess around with her. If we're not going to get Polly with her, bring her in for a session. I don't need somebody in love with an enemy of America working The Run."

Abigail pinched her inner thigh to fight off the sudden fatigue. She knew better than to let Rice speak very much -before his voice could have its way with her. Stay awake, she thought. "I'm not sure that's the best idea." Abigail blinked slowly, lifting her eyelids as if they weighed a ton each.

"Good thing I don't give a fuck about what you think."

"Then why ask my opinion of Jo at all?"

"Information is power. Need to know what I'm up against."

"Me telling you something is a bad idea is information, motherfucker." Probably not the smartest thing to say to her boss, but when she grew this tired, when she fought off the hypnosis this hard, she turned to the cranky side.

"Touché."

"Jo's got a loyalty streak in her, long as a Nebraska highway. Which means she's got a vengeance streak, too. Until you know her a little better, I don't think you should underestimate her." The smoke from the clove cigarette caught in the back of her throat, and she coughed the familiar hack that'd become so prevalent. "I saw her take out three guys outside of Reno, just to prove she could. And she's a natural with weapons. She could be an army unto herself if she ever figured out how lethal she is."

"So, you're suggesting I let an army unto herself wander freely along The Run? This one-person army whom you previously stated was still in love with somebody actively trying to shut us down."

"I'm suggesting no such thing. I'm suggesting you take a little extra caution with this one." Abigail wanted the next sentence to sound tough, but it came out corny. "This one's special, but I've got my eye on her for you."

Deacon Rice disappeared back into the shade of the limo. "Bring her to me, Abigail. Soon." The window raised. The engine revved. The limo pulled away, leaving Abigail wondering what to do next.

Circumstances allowed her little time to ponder her move, though. As the limo's taillights dimmed and disappeared over the off-ramp, a new vehicle puttered into the rest stop – a good, old-fashioned yellow cab. Blood rushed to Abigail's head and the weight of concern lifted. She had to choke back the tears begging to flow, but the smile grew so big it threatened to break her face. Again, she flashed her headlights.

Jo climbed into the Mack's cab, shoulders slumped, she sulking, spirit somber. She tried putting on a brave face, but tears streaked her cheeks and new ones puddled when Abs made eye contact.

"I'm sorry, young lass."

"No you're not."

Abigail started the truck. "I'm sorry you're hurting. I'm happy as hell for me, though."

"Yeah. I understand. Thanks."

"She didn't show?"

"I felt like an ass. I waited way too long." Jo wiped her nose with the back of her trembling hand and sniffed. "I just wanted to be the one to say it was over, you know?"

"If it makes you feel any better, I waited just as long for you, right?"

Jo nodded. "I should've listened to you. I didn't want to believe she'd hurt me even more."

"She's a manipulative bitch. She took advantage of you when you were weak." Abigail placed her hand on Jo's knee. Jo grabbed the hand and squeezed. "World's full of people like that, and it has nothing to do with you. She'll get what she's got coming someday."

Jo blew out a long, defeated breath and pulled the pink hair from her eyes. "Well, I'm all yours now, Abs. What's next?"

Abigail put the truck in gear and motored out of the rest stop. They headed for the nearest Money Run artery.

# # #

November 2007 – same day. In back of a taxi, cruising Manhattan:

Jo's iPhone rang, some cello piece as its ringtone. Polly answered.

"It's not safe still. Rice's henchman ain't leaving 'til Jo does."

"How's she look?" Polly asked.

"Pissed. Sad. Pretty hot except for that nose."

Polly could see the Empire State Building, contemplated how she could get to the roof. Her heart ached at being so close. "Any chance you can get a message to her, David?"

"Not without tipping off that big-ass motherfucker. He manages to stay within earshot at all times."

"Shit."

"How long do I have to wait here, Polly? It's freaking cold."

"Stay until she leaves. Let me know when she does." Polly hung up.

The taxi turned again, going down the same avenue they'd traversed dozens of times while Polly tried waiting out Deacon Rice's man. The fare clicked again and had reached well into three digits. Polly stuck her nose out the rolled-down window to avoid the cigar smoke. Puffs of chilled vapor escaped her nostrils. The sounds of traffic helped drown out the sappy love songs the cabbie had listened to all afternoon.

"Listen lady, my shift's over. I don't get home, my wife is gonna use my balls for ping-pong practice." They stopped at a red light. "Why don't you just pay me and get another taxi? I'll help you out with that thing."

Polly ruminated on it for a moment. Nodded her head slightly.

The cab pulled to the curb to a chorus of angry horns alerting them to how many lanes the driver cut off with his maneuver. She and the driver exited. When the old, bald, white guy and his stinky cigar went around to the other side to remove the cello she'd bought for Jo, Polly bolted, blending into the masses traversing the sidewalk. Crying as she ran.

# # #

May 2006. Taking out the trailer park trash:

Jo was pretty sure she'd broken the little fucker's knee cap. Whether she had or not didn't much matter. He wasn't going to be a problem, and she was left free to finish what she'd came to the trailer park for: get her money back from the Asian bitch. Take out a little interest from the cunt's hide.

The Winnebago door remained open, yellow light spilling into street like a sick ooze. The adrenaline from disposing of the two strangers left her body abuzz with energy. She wondered if it was bloodlust, or just plain lust.

Jo belched. The burn from the moonshine vapor rested in the back of her throat, and she swallowed it back down, regretting it immediately. Stumbling into the light as if the glow sucked her in, she was drunk and half ready to kill. Ready to fuck. Ready to fucking kill.

Jo thrust the pointed end of her broken fretboard into the opening, trying to catch any surprises the light might have obscured. After verifying nothing occupied her blind spot, she barrel-rolled into the RV. In a maneuver that impressed even her drunk ass, she landed on her feet, weapons at the ready, and more alert than a one-third-gallon jug of moonshine should have left her.

And there stood Polly.

A silk robe, kimono style, with no tie hid nothing. Damn, Jo thought, this Asian fetish is going to get me in trouble someday, and knew it was that day. But thinking back to her garage, to the letter from Julliard that claimed her deposit never arrived, brought Jo's focus back. She might have beat the ever-loving shit out of the midget and his companion, but things were about to get serious.

"So you know, right?" Polly pulled the robe closed, but still kept her manicured vagina visible. "You're a regular Nancy Drew."

"Know?"

"Yeah. I ain't going to lie, Josephine. It was me."

"Nooooooo. I can't believe it." Jo slurred the words, but the sarcasm still shone through, bright as a drunken nova. "And you call me Josephine one more time, I'm gonna shove this fretboard so far up your ass, I could tune it by twisting your ear."

"Look, I get the hostility--"

"That comforts me." Jo spotted the humorously large dildo on the floor. Thought she might shove it up the bitch's ass after she cut her from stem to stern – before she died, but well into the bleeding out process.

"How'd you figure it was me?" Polly fiddled with the kimono's hem and shifted her weight from foot to foot in a swaying, flirting gesture. Jo couldn't deny it was distracting. "I thought it'd look like a hate crime and you'd come running to the one person who could understand you."

"Nobody else cared enough to do it. I was going to be out of their hair in a day."

"Exactly. So you see, I care. You matter to me." Jo had no explanation for why that sentence stung so much. "I wouldn't have done it if I had another choice." Polly didn't physically defend herself at all. Her sense of comfort irritated Jo.

"You had to break my DVDs? You had no choice? You had to piss on my floor? No – no fucking choice involved there."

"Yeah, that's my bad. I was covering my tracks." Polly took a step forward, and allowed her left breast to pop free. "A bit overzealous, I guess, but you get me worked up. I'll replace all that shit. I promise you."

"You pissed on my stuff. You pissed on Cynthia Rothrock."

"I kind of hoped you were into that." Polly's laugh would have been disheartening if it weren't so insulting. Still, her confidence made Jo second guess if she held the right.

"You stole my money. You broke Beatrice! How could you do that? You stole my fucking future." Sweat poured from Jo in sheets. A burst of spittle accompanied each word.

"I'm offering you a future. Jo, I came a long way to meet you, and if I leave alone, there's not much reason for me to go on." Polly circled Jo, lightly touching her on the back as she passed. "Your money's safe. You can have it all back and more, just hear me out."

Jo whipped the broken fretboard, snapped it back. The D-string popped, tearing her impromptu nunchucks in two. Then Jo dropped. Crumpled on the floor, she let the tears flow. Or would have had she had any left.

"I wouldn't have done it, Jo, if I had any other way. I tried the nice way, but I'm desperate. Dozens of those motherfuckers are hunting me." Polly pointed to the alleyway where Lefty struggled to pull his companion into the Cadillac. "And they're the C-team."

"Why me? I just want to be left alone."

"You see what you did to those two?"

"All of this because you want me to beat somebody up for you?"

"Kind of, yeah." Polly's smile cut through the fog in Jo's mind, and Jo's seething dropped a few dozen degrees. The Asian woman hit play on a boom-box resting on the stove. Christina Aguilera's "Beautiful" started on a low volume. Polly knelt and encased Jo in her arms.

"Jo, I need you. I'm no crazy stalker, but you, missing a Y chromosome, win a regional championship in wrestling crazy Iowa? That's going to hit my radar." Polly reached for the bat. "I know all about you Jo. I ain't afraid of you because I know you better than you do. This is my life's work, I'm a recruiter."

"For what? The cunt army?"

"Sergeant Cunnilingus at your service." Polly tossed the bat aside.

"Give me a single reason not to break every bone in your damn body." From outside, she heard the Caddy's engine roar and "Strawberry Letter 23" began in mid-song. The tune faded as the car drove away.

"Because I'm a lot more fun with those bones intact." Polly smoothed Jo's hair and sang along with the boom-box in a low, surprisingly good voice. She kissed her forehead. "We can do great things. I'm not exaggerating when I say together, we can change the world."

"I can never trust you."

"Name one soul who deserves that." Using her kimono sleeve, Polly dabbed at Jo's cheeks. The mascara stained the white satin.

Jo felt exhausted. Defeated. Yet somehow safe. "You'll do whatever it takes to get what you want. I know that much about you."

"Maybe I do it to a greater degree, but I think everybody suffers that particular trait."

"You even a real lesbian? Is this just part of your way to fuck with me?" Jo raised her head and looked Polly straight in the eyes. "I need you to be honest about this much."

"No, not exactly a lesbian." Her million-dollar smile flashed again. "I'm tri-sexual. I'll try anything." Polly leaned in for the kiss.

Jo accepted it eagerly.

Over each of the many times making love that night, Jo dropped her guard a little more and Polly explained a lot more. About the Money Run and its sustainability due to corporate greed and people willing to look the other way. About the PAGANS and their resistance. That if they, Polly and her, could disrupt the Money Run, they could return economic power to the people – freedom fighters on par with the founding fathers.

Jo thought most of it bullshit, but appreciated Polly's enthusiasm for her tales. She appreciated more the idea that she'd take her away from Maxville. They agreed on a one-week trial under the condition that Jo would have all her money returned, her DVDs replaced and a new cello. Especially the cello. And if she were to be honest with herself, Jo looked forward to the adventure, but she wasn't going to change her name as the other PAGANS did. It was time to find herself, and she couldn't do that pretending to be somebody else.

In the light of dawn creeping through the Winnebago's windows, they held each other. The beginning of a bad-ass hangover bubbled and brewed inside Jo's rumbling belly.

"Before I forget, thank you, Jo."

"For not killing you?"

"Well, that. But thanks for getting here when you did." Polly lightly ran her fingers over Jo's belly. "I don't think there's enough therapy in the universe to overcome getting raped by a one-armed dwarf."

"That'd be a tough one to explain, I guess."

Polly drew over the design of the Yo Ma-Ma tattoo on Jo's forearm. "Is this supposed to be gangsta' for a Maxvillian?"

"No. Had to go the big city for that."

"What, Sioux Falls?"

"No – the BIG city. Des Moines." Jo took a long draw from a water jug. Despite not being cold, the re-hydration kept the lurking hangover at bay. "It was supposed to say 'Yo-Yo Ma.' You know, the cellist?"

Polly was trying to suppress a giggle. Unsuccessfully.

"Apparently expecting a back alley Des Moines tattoo artist to get the cultural reference was too much to ask. So, Yo Ma-Ma it is."

With that, the pair broke into uncontrollable laughter. Something they'd share often over the next few months as Polly proved the existence of The Run to Jo, and Jo accepted her own role in destroying it.

# # #

March 2008. Jo meets The Wizard:

The fight in this one impressed Deacon Rice. The pure balls she'd displayed by knocking on his door, coming to him instead of being sent for, proved her backbone consisted of steel and resolve. Of course, Lefty alerting him she was on her way provided the warning he'd needed for his special surprise, and she'd walked into the Taser before uttering a full sentence.

Except for the nose, she was a fine looking young thing, too. Tight in all the right places. A nose job from Doc Edsel would remedy the honker, though, maybe toss in a tit touch-up while she was under. Deacon Rice displayed his sermon smile, and understood he gazed upon a cash cow.

As long as the persuasion immersion was taking, and they were well into their second day, she'd proved to possess a strong mind, too. Several times, he thought he'd had her. The familiar glazed expression clouded her eyes, but she wouldn't respond to commands. Instead, she'd drift away fifteen to twenty minutes each episode, as if her mind had simply vacated her body, before returning, ready to fight his mind games afresh.

He bent to the chair she was tied to. Under the sole lit lamp shining in the vast, vacated warehouse, he utilized the acoustics to create an echo effect. "You there, Miss Jo?" The deacon kept his voice steady at its pleasant comforting monotone.

Her eyes said no, but the loogie she planted straight across his prosthetic nose told him yes.

"You still planning on killing me, or are you just looking to get out alive, now?"

"Oh, I'm killing you, motherfucker."

"Awww. Here I thought we might be friends."

"Not sure we'd run in the same social circles. I don't lie with snakes."

He dabbed away the phlegm with a silk handkerchief, white, of course. "I'm a snake now?" Deacon wished to keep engaged in conversation as long as possible. Every word he verbalized presented another opportunity to lure her under his charms. "Very well." He flicked his tongue at her. "What type of slimy reptilian serpent would I be?"

Jo blinked. Slowly. She didn't answer. The far-away look crossed her eyes. Deacon Rice had learned over the two days, though, and recognized she hadn't submitted. Using a new tactic, he hit the transistor radio's power. The music shocked her from whatever trance she'd begun falling under. That's a helpful strategy, thought the deacon.

"Oh, how apropos."

Stealers Wheel's "Stuck in the Middle With You" blasted from the ancient radio. Deacon Rice lowered the volume, removed his handy icepick from his inside suit pocket, and broke into the famous Michael Madsen cha-cha. He twirled the icepick around his middle finger. The glare Jo shot him communicated her desire to peel the skin clean from his face. He moved closer to taunt her and sung the lyrics in his unique style, hypnotic voice and all, thinking he might as well try the approach as nothing else had panned out.

Then, she shot her leg out and kicked him square in the giblets.

Deacon Rice answered with a left that knocked the chair over. The sound of Jo's head banging against the cement floor resembled a solid home run from the steroid era. In the warehouse, the knock rang out over and over. The glazed look re-appeared on his quarry's face, and the deacon breathed in relief. If he could control his voice, he'd have her, but the agony throbbing between his thighs overrode everything. His next decision decided the fate of the Money Run, and cost him Jo as a sex slave. Still, he'd gain her as an assassin.

He placed the icepick in Jo's hand, closed her fingers around it. She needed to pay. Usually, he performed the lobotomies himself. Over the decades, he'd perfected the technique and could do the trick with one flick of the wrist. But this bitch, she didn't deserve the quick painless way. She'd brought all this on herself and needed to understand. Needed lessons in respect.

"Take it Jo." The words fell from his mouth with great effort. The anger and pain made it difficult for him to maintain his usual focus, but he had to strike while she was dazed. "I won't hurt you. No ma'am. Going to do it for yourself. Any half lucid moments, for the rest of your life, you'll think back to this next five minutes. See yourself shoving the pick into your eye duct." He paused for a breath and to slow down. "You'll hear the wet insertion and feel the blade enter your cerebral cortex. You'll remember how you couldn't help but twist your hand and how you yourself carved out your very soul." He re-started singing the lyrics to the song.

When Jo raised the pick, directed it at her head, Deacon Rice relaxed. It'd been a difficult and long persuasion, but as always, he'd won out. "Do it, Jo. Do it. Do it. Do it."

Jo's arm trembled. Her expression strained and she growled like an agitated pit bull. Eyes bulged. Face reddened.

Deacon Rice allowed a relieved breath.

Jo shifted her eyes from the pick to his face. She grinned, and Rice's stomach dropped into his bowels.

"Do it, Do it, doitdoitdoitdoitfuckingdoit."

Jo's grin cemented. The icepick shook in her hand, but no longer aimed at her eye duct. However, the grin turned to an expression of concern as the metal inched closer. Concern washed over Deacon Rice, as well. This wasn't what he instructed. "Your eye, Jo. Your eye. Stab the icepick into the duct, twist and succumb."

Jo's free arm grabbed the wrist of the arm under the deacon's control.

Waves of wooziness hit Deacon Rice, as if his voice's energy repelled against him – bounced off his intended target and he was half-hypnotizing his own self.

Gerry Rafferty's lyrics waved in louder and calmer volumes. "Do it!" But the deacon couldn't gage how the command came out. He suffered for consciousness himself.

"Do it, do it, do it."

Jo held the pick away with her off hand. Again, she spat at Deacon Rice and smirked like she knew something nobody else could.

"Do it, do it, do it."

"Yes." Jo raised the icepick. Screamed. Brought the pick down with a violent thrust. Turned her head. Pierced her eardrum, and she squealed like an angel burning in hell. "Your voice won't have power over me!"

Before the deacon could act, she pulled the pick free with a wet swoosh, flashed her head around and stabbed through her other ear. Blood splattered over Rice's white suit, hit his face, landed in his mouth, and soaked his pompadour. He'd never forget the screams. Never.

He'd also never meet another person so focused on freedom as Jo, and realized he'd have to keep her from PAGANS at any price.

"Fair enough." He paid close attention to see if Jo understood. Shook his head in disbelief when she did. She writhed and slithered through the pooling blood, hands covering her ears as if trying to keep her brain inside. "I'll have Abigail pick you up. We're done for today, but we're not finished. Not by a long fuckin shot."

# # #

Independence Day, 2008: No turning back:

For clarity's sake, everyone should understand: Jo Martindale was a natural. The moral ambiguity of The Run fitted her like a high-end hand-tailored designer gown. She no longer turned the other cheek as her father had preached in miserable Maxville. Instead, the social construct of this new world allowed – hell, demanded – retribution on an escalated scale. Unlike Maxville, Jo understood the rules here. Or thought she did. Enough to get by, anyway.

Abigail had been oddly quiet for the drive, honestly, for the week. Her chain smoking had gone from one after another to a couple cigarettes lit at all times. The cab stank like rancid pumpkin pie and sweat.

But not sex. And Jo couldn't understand why not.

"We gonna talk about this, Abs?"

"If we have to." She blew a plume of clove smoke out the window. "And if you think we do, then we have to."

"I'm in your world, okay? I gave. I fucking stayed with you."

Abigail clenched the wheel tighter. Her fingers went white. Smacking her lips a couple of times, she attempted her consoling smile, but couldn't control the cough that ended with a moist splash in Jo's face. "I'm not sure I want this for you, Jo. You can do better." She turned her attention from the road and made sure Jo could see her lips clearly. "A lot better."

"Depends on your definition of better."

Abs reached and rubbed Jo's thigh, allowed a comforting squeeze even though her smile conveyed anything but comfort. "Everything you've done up to now – you've done for survival." Another coughing fit hit Abs. The tears might have been from that, but most likely not. "You do this, it's for profit. You do this, you go from sympathetic to vindictive. You go assassin."

"Yeah. Bout sums it up." She grabbed Abigail's hand and squeezed as if she could provide solace. "We have a problem, Abs?"

Abigail down shifted. The washboard of the dirt road shook the Mack's cab like a Parkinson's patient with a Magic 8-Ball. "We have no problems. I'm sorry, Jo. I'm truly, really fucking sorry, young lass."

"I don't know what for."

Abigail wouldn't tell her everything, and Jo understood that was part of The Run, but watching how terribly it ate away at Abs hurt Jo more than saying goodbye to her former self.

"I guess it's just, like, I don't know. Like if I gave a friend drugs for the first time, wanted to share the fun with them, you know? Then watching that friend turn into an addict. I had no intention of you taking this role."

"Quit mothering me, Abs." Although, deep down, Jo appreciated the mothering.

Abigail said something, but turned her head away, and Jo couldn't tell if it was intentional. Lip reading had come easily to Jo. Being an outsider back home, eating alone in the student cafeteria and everybody keeping as far away so as not to catch The Gay, she'd practiced watching townsfolk mouth words for years, usually with heartbreaking results. She observed her parents enjoy countless meals through the kitchen window while she prepared something on the hotplate in her garage. Rarely did Jo ever come up in the topic of those dinner conversations.

For the first two months after Jo's session with Deacon Rice, Abigail would spend hours practicing with her. They figured it'd be easier than sign language. Operating an eighteen wheeler didn't offer so many chances for such expression, not even with Abigail's advanced driving skill set.

The Mack diesel came to a stop at a T in the road. Abs faced Jo. "Last chance, young lass. You say the word and I'll drive your happy ass back to Idaho right now."

"Iowa."

"That's what I said."

Jo couldn't argue with her. She might well have been wrong, although she felt ninety percent sure of what she'd seen. She flipped the visor down and checked her nose in the mirror, ran her fingers over all the crooked ridges. "I'm going to look so much better for you." In her peripheral vision, she saw Abigail respond, but feigned ignorance. "You say this Doc Edsel's aces at this cosmetic surgery, right?"

Abigail jabbed her in the ribs. When Jo turned, she saw the tears streaking her partner's cheeks.

"Don't do this for me. I don't want this on what's left of my conscience."

"What else am I going to do, Abs? I'm a deaf-ass cellist without a cello. I ain't got friend one outside of The Run, and if I go back, that Asian cunt is going to hunt me down and I don't think I could stop myself. She's got some weird power over me."

"You just like Asian chicks."

"Who doesn't?"

"Gay Asian men?"

"More for us, then."

That crack brought a smirk to her Abs' face. "I'll never be able to talk you out of anything, will I?" She ran her fingers through Jo's hair.

"I get talked into shit. Too damn stubborn to be talked out of it, though." Jo kissed Abigail's hand.

The Mack lurched forward, down an even thinner dirt road. The corn stalks hadn't yielded any harvest yet, as it was too early in the season. Still, it seemed like the plants were watching them.

Without warning or any sign, the field opened up. Macadam and Jerry-rigged Christmas lights formed a makeshift air strip. At the far end of the runway, a single semi stood parked, cargo door open and ramp down. Somebody napped on the ramp.

"There he it's," Abigail said. Jo figured the final word was "is." "Chad Banderas."

"Victim number one."

"He's a small-time bookie, least by The Run standards." Abigail tossed her cigarette out the window and, to Jo's surprise, didn't automatically reach for another. "Rice claims the maroon's been skimming about six-thousand a month from the midget-tossing tournaments."

"He wants me to off him over six G?"

"A month. Most likely it's not him the Deacon has the problem with. I'd venture this is more of a message to some bigger fish."

"Still, the amount he's paying me, to stop six-thousand? You sure this deacon is the business man everyone makes him out to be?"

"He's a lot of bad things, but the fuckstick knows his business."

Seeing the guy brought it home to Jo, and for the first time she thought she wouldn't be able to follow through with her assignment. A ball formed in her gut, heavy and solid as lead, and dryness filled her mouth. Abigail again put her hand on Jo's thigh and squeezed. She then put the Mack in drive and headed for destiny.

As they approached, tremors ran through Jo's hands. She fought off the urge nagging for her to return to her inside place.

The Mack parked next to the other semi. Chad Banderas didn't even remove the ball cap covering his eyes.

Jo's heart beat so hard, it was visible beneath her Misfits t-shirt. Abigail bent to kiss her. "Go get 'em, tiger."

"That's your pep speech?"

"Best I got." She pecked Jo on the cheek, wiped away the lipstick and kissed her again on the mouth.

Jo checked her Colt .45 and stuck it down the back of her Levi's. Her hands shook so frenetically, she had difficulty finding the door latch. Outside, the heat hit like a blanket trying to suffocate her. The sweat she'd worked up flowed more freely.

The bookie still hadn't moved. While Jo'd roughed up a few Run inhabitants, seeing him there, unpro-tected, added weight to the ball bulging in her belly. Suddenly, she had to shit, and a rage swelled inside her. How dare this cocksucker make her feel this way. She mule-kicked the metal ramp with malicious intention.

Chad Banderas removed the cap from his face, swirled a toothpick around his mouth and spat. He said something, but the amount of chaw residing in his low-er lip prevented Jo from translating.

"Deacon Rice says your showing up light." Jo hoped her voice conveyed confidence.

Banderas said something else. Again unintelligible.

Jo kicked the ramp again. She swallowed to keep her heart from escaping through her throat. "Time's too late to make it up."

The cloud of confusion across the man's face confirmed Jo had no idea what the guy was saying. He stood. Towering over Jo by a head and a half, he moved in as close as possible without touching her. Why do all the fuckers on the Run have to be so goddamned big, Jo thought. Again, the man spat, and a brown glob splattered on Jo's Adidas.

She looked from her shoe to his face. His head blocked out the sun. Doubt again crept into her thoughts. Until she saw the ball cap more clearly. It advertised the same farm equipment company as the octogenarian homophobe's hat back in Maxville. Banderas sported similar suspenders, as well, just like old Walter. Jo pushed away doubt and let the familiar anger run through her like fire through dry grass.

She shoved the behemoth square in the chest. It only moved him half a step back, but provided all the room she'd need. Jo leapt. The roundhouse kick bounced off the side of his head. While in mid-air, she grabbed his thigh for balance, slipped her other leg around the back of his head, scissoring his neck, and pulled Banderas to the tarmac. She drove his head into the runway.

He clawed at her thighs. Jo locked her ankles, squeezed her legs around his neck. As his face reddened, and chaw flew everywhere, Jo only saw Walter's wrinkled-ass puss. Jo squeezed harder. She heard the old man call her Lezzy Jo in the back of her mind, then saw Sandy's face, her eyes telling Jo she'd never be as good as any of the Gurleys. Jo reached for the morphing head, grabbed around the back and dug her thumbs into the eye sockets. She wished she could hear the shrieks.

As she thought back to all the injustices suffered throughout her life, her grip turned tighter. Chad's left eye popped like a deformed zit. Gelatin and blood greased her fingers. The fight in him weakened. The adrenaline coursed through Jo, and she realized her face hurt from smiling. Moments after the other eye popped, Banderas went limp.

Jo released him. She found her feet and stared at her hands. Then the vomit flew.

When she returned to the Mack's cab, Abigail held out a machete for her. "Deacon needs proof. Crazy fucker wants his trophy."

Jo nodded and accepted the blade.

# # #

February, 2013. Goodbye for good. Probably:

Jo slipped into her leather jacket. She thought the plan was too stupid to work, but also knew she'd never really hurt Polly, and that left her no other option. She screwed the adapter from her breastplate onto the hose that ran the length of her left arm, an odd vein beneath the skin with an outlet valve at the wrist bone.

"You're not going to bolt once I unrig the door, are you?"

"Deacon Rice is expecting me to come back with your head. I show up empty handed, and I'm suddenly unemployed." She tossed Polly the rest of her clothes, and they landed at her feet. "Besides, you still owe me a lot of money."

Polly said something else.

"I have to see you when you talk," Jo said.

Polly faced Jo. "Sorry. That's going to take some getting used to."

"We're not going to be together long enough for you to get used to it."

"You've gotten mean in your old age." Polly turned back to the door, and yanked the network of crazy wire spaghetti with one hand.

Jo jumped. "What the fuck?"

"I don't know how to rig this shit, Jo. That's what I got guys like you for." She tossed the benign wires at Jo's feet and unbolted the locks. "Told your bitch ass I was just a recruiter."

For a second, Jo thought of frying Polly right there. But looking at her, dressed only in a Spongebob Squarepants' thong, made Jo ache with lust, and the thought squirreled away. Undoubtedly, Polly had delayed dressing, understanding the power she held over Jo.

"Get the shack ready while I get dressed, would you? Let's blow this popsicle stand."

Jo agreed and stacked the remaining firewood and coal atop the worn rug. She threw the few books not previously used for fuel onto the pile, and noticed they comprised the entirety of Frank Lauria's Doctor Orient series. Saving the best for last, Jo thought.

The shadow cast by the yellow hanging bulb illuminating Polly approaching from behind, a ginormous blade at the ready. Jo inhaled deeply, preparing for what came next. She spun, ready to eject the Yo Ma-Ma blade.

"Let's get this over with." Polly presented the scimitar for Jo. On her other arm, a moth-riddled towel hung as if she were a butler presenting tea.

"You got everything you're taking?"

"Backpack's by the door."

Jo accepted the short sword. "This is it, you know. Your PAGANS days are over."

Rubbing her arms as if a sudden chill hit her, Polly paused, then nodded. She looked around the shack. "This is what my PAGAN days have got me."

"You ever going to tell me why you named it PAGANS?"

"We never talked about that?" Polly looked at her fingers, extending each one so in order to spell out the F-U-C-K D-A-L-E – right pinkie finger to left pinkie finger.

"Well, I was drunk most of the time we spent together, but I don't think we breached that topic."

"PAGANS – Patriots Against Government And National Socialism." She couldn't keep a straight face as she mouthed the words.

"But...What the fuck? You're as socialist as Sweden."

"Hey, anagrams are hard, okay?" She laughed, but with little spirit.

At that second, Jo would have given five years of her life to hear Polly's old laugh again.

Polly, Jo's-once-sweet-now-defeated Polly, knelt by the stove. She placed her protracted left pinkie, adorned with the letter "E," on the bricks that made up the hearth.

"No," Jo said. "The 'A.'"

Polly looked up. "Always sending a message, huh?" She extended her middle finger, flashed it at Jo before planting the digit across the brick. She turned her head away.

Jo raised the scimitar. "Sorry, Polly. This was your idea, though." And Jo was thankful she couldn't hear the screams.

#

Jo had packed the Prius, her former Prius, with Polly and her bandaged hand wrapped in a towel that she'd soaked in the snow. She'd recovered as much ammo and munitions from the Duster as she could find, also including Polly's supply of C4, and had spent far too long searching for the UFO eight-track tape among the wreckage to no avail. The severed finger rested in a lunchbox-sized plastic cooler beneath Polly's feet in the passenger-side foot well.

After returning from removing the spike strip that caused her crash and giving the shack a final onceover, Jo stood just outside the open door. She waited for the pressure to build in the hose, then unscrewed the valve in her wrist. A jerk of her middle finger triggered the ignitor, and a stream of flame shot through the doorway and kissed the pile atop the rug. Jo felt the singe take her eyebrows. She'd used enough gasoline to insure the shed would be nothing but a pile of ashes, but still wished she had a body to leave. Surely the Deacon would investigate if she didn't sell her story well enough.

She sprinted for the Prius, hit the ignition, and headed back on the road she'd entered from. The nearest hospital was hours away, and Polly'd lose a lot of blood before they'd arrive. Jo worried shock might set in, and that kept her foot full down on the accelerator.

The Prius had seen better days. Driving it again proved a surreal experience, and nips of nostalgia taunted Jo. She couldn't recognize the vibrations from the music playing for a long while before realizing it was Dvorak.

Polly's head lilted toward her. "I got something for you." With her good hand, she opened the glove box, and brought out a piece of paper. "Every cent of it. Made out to you. I knew that cocksucker would send you." She handed Jo the cashier's check and drifted off to sleep. The "to" line read "Josephine Martindale."

Jo let the tears flow for the rest of the drive. She knew Polly wouldn't turn her back on PAGANS, and if she popped up on Deacon Rice's radar again, it would be the end of Jo's time on The Run. She hoped Polly could remain incognito for enough years for Jo to live a good life. Finish killing some more motherfuckers because she loved it so much.

Goddamned Asian fetish, she thought. Always knew it'd be the death of me.

# # #

September, 2012. Edsel's on The Nines. Dream wedding:

"Are you sure about this, Jo?" Doc Edsel asked. "She's gone. The Vanilla Ice thing died with her."

Jo nodded. Even if she didn't want the surgery, she needed it. She'd come to depend on them like Abs had been with her nasty-ass clove cigarettes. The first thing entering her mind every morning was a calculation as to how long until she could last before going under the knife again. If she didn't have that to look forward to, she'd never get out of bed. "As long as the Deacon's footing the bill,

I'll be coming back. Might want to think about a regular appointment with me."

"Okay. I'll try and get this done before the storm moves in. Get you on your way so you're not trapped here for a couple of days."

Doc Edsel placed the anesthesia mask in place. Jo breathed in the heavenly gas.

"Count backwards from ten." Doc put his surgical mask on, as well.

But Jo didn't even make it to nine before falling under. For the first time, she'd meet Abigail in death.

Back at the Pit, Jo could hear again. Abigail sang Christina Aguilera's "Beautiful," but for some reason it was in Polly's voice. A wreath of wild flowers sat like a tiara on Abigail's gray hair, and she held a bouquet of dead weeds as she strode down the bowling alley approach. Dwarfs arched over her from both sides, a new one launching with each step, flying in slow motion. Abs wore her wedding overalls. Her smile was so big, it nearly broke her face.

Deacon Rice presided. But his voice wasn't the hypnotic, measured cadence. Instead, he sounded like Gilbert Godfried on helium. Each syllable he uttered made Jo long for her deafness.

The sluts of honor were the prom-queen wanna-bes from miserable Maxwell. The best man was Sandy Gurley, except she was five-hundred pounds. And fifteen-years old. With Deacon Rice's ice pick between her teeth.

"We'll be together long past our physical lives, Jo." Abigail talked without moving her lips, and her appealing voice was a welcome respite from the grind of Deacon Rice's.

And in a flash, the deacon broke into the wedding scene from "The Princess Bride."

While he talked about twue wuv, Jo felt something between her legs. Something very pleasant. When she looked down, her gown, made from diamonds, had split to the crotch. Polly's decapitated head lapped her pussy like a puppy welcoming her home. She spoke in some Asian tongue, and what a tongue it was.

"I do. Fucking-A, I do," Jo said. Which was her exact response during her and Abs' actual wedding.

Somehow, with no reason, they were in the Mack's cab, and as usual, Jo felt relieved to no longer be in Deacon Rice's presence. Behind them, a mob of ice pick wielding dwarfs pursued. They sung Strawberry Letter 23, but in the deacon's voice. Still, she was with Abigail again. She was whole.

Together, they drove off the edge of the horizon.

#

March, 2013. A date with the deacon:

There should be no question: Jo Martindale knew she'd walked willingly into the lions' den, a juicy porterhouse hanging from her neck. Was aware of Deacon Rice's anxiety over Polly Amorous' existence, and he'd be on high alert for any possible hijinks. What Jo hoped for was his overzealousness at Polly's demise would make him a little more susceptible to her story, simply because he wanted it to be true.

She dropped the cooler on his desk.

"Surely you jest, Ms. Polly." He pulled the cooler closer to him. "Her head couldn't fit in this."

"Things didn't go as planned."

The deacon swallowed hard, like he could keep his temper bottled up by doing so. "You don't say." With his pock-marked face, perfectly coiffed silver pompadour and funky plastic nose, he appeared even more menacing than your average crime boss. He looked like he could kill you with kindness or a claw hammer, either way, without losing a wink of sleep and a smug expression of satisfaction.

"Bitch had the drop on me. You know by now, you could only find her when she wanted to be found." Jo talked slowly and concentrated on using the past tense. Any slip might send him off. "She was waiting." She pointed to her black eye for evidence. "I had to torch her. There was nothing left of her head. I was lucky to get what I got for you. By the time I was done, there were only scraps left."

Deacon Rice slid the cooler lid back. His poker face revealed nothing, but Jo felt the temperature in the room drop. He removed the paper towel from the cooler, it now pink from the blood diluted in the ice. Unrolling the package, he broke into a smile that was anything but happy. The finger plopped on his desk. Deacon Rice picked it up, examined it, and licked the end that'd been severed. "So the torch works to your satisfaction, then?"

"Doc Edsel did us up right. He always does."

"For what he charges, he damn sure better." The deacon spun in his chair, faced out the window overlooking Chesapeake Bay. If he said anything, obviously Jo didn't know. He stayed that way for a long, awkward amount of time, and Jo wondered if she'd been dismissed. She looked to his bodyguard, Ash, who stood stationed at the door. He shook his head in the negative, and Jo mouthed "thank you" to him.

When Rice finally turned back around, his familiar, bullshit grin graced his face. "And now we confront an existence without Polly Amorous. I doubt them fucking PAGANS stick together long enough to see out the summer."

He pulled open the bottom drawer on his mahogany desk. Onto the blotter, he deposited two fistfuls of bound hundred-dollar bills. And then two more.

"Thank you for your work, Jo. I knew you had it in you."

"Thank you, Deacon." Jo reached for her payment, but the Deacon grabbed her by the wrist. She expected the gesture to be followed by the ice pick impaling her.

"One more thing." He released her arm and reached into the inside pocket of his white, silk suit.

A flashback to the last time he'd done so jolted Jo. Again, she felt sure the ice pick would come into play somehow. Instead, he removed a fob with a Ford Mustang emblem hanging from the keychain. "I'm sorry about the Duster. I know how much you loved that car. Consider this a bonus. Doing in Polly surely warrants one." He slid the keychain across the blotter.

Jo swallowed her heart back down to its proper resting place. "Thank you so, much, sir."

"It's in the parking garage." Deacon Rice took a bite off of Polly's finger. "I get served so many fingers, you'd think they were all the women of The Run were made of. Just a bunch of finger people."

Jo didn't know how to respond. She chose not to.

"Ash will show you to your new car." He dumped the remaining cooler ice in the trash bin and placed the money inside. "I'll be in contact soon for a new assignment. Give Doc Edsel my best."

Jo followed Ash from the room. As Ash was a mute, thanks to Deacon's little ice pick trick, the two didn't even try to communicate until he showed her to her new car, a blood-red 2013 Mustang. Jo put on her best excited act, but it felt forced. She still half-expected the other shoe to drop.

Ash opened the door for her and shook her hand. He grabbed it firmly and glared at her with his remaining good eye. With the handshake, he passed her a note scribbled in the worst chicken-scratch Jo'd ever seen. It consisted of two words, or as near to words as his lobotomy-addled brain allowed:

"hE nOs."

THE FUCKING END!

\# \# \#

Acknowledgements

Writing means spending a ton of time alone. However, one of the rewards, in fact in the darkest hours when the story seems to be coming irretrievably undone, perhaps the only reward, is the unity one feels others who've done it or those who support the idiocy of it all. As such, I owe the following comrades big sweaty hugs, but I'm sure they'd prefer merely my appreciation. So, Kurt Dinan, John Mantooth, Gene O'Neill, Erik Williams, John Palisano, Petra Miller, Shane McKenzie, John Langan, Sean Eads, Linda Anderson, Dirk Anderson, Abram Dress, Carter Wilson and Stephen Graham Jones – thank you. Sweaty hugs to come.

About Sam W. Anderson

Sam W. Anderson lives in Denver, Colorado with his wife, two kids and the most expensive rescue mutt in history. He's the author of over forty published short stories and collaborative novels, and two short-story collections: POSTCARDS FROM PURGATORY, and AMERICAN GOMORRAH: THE MONEY RUN OMNIBUS. The latter will be updated and reissued from Rothco Press. THE NINES is his first solo novel. He likes pie.

CPSIA information can be obtained
at www.ICGtesting.com
Printed in the USA
LVHW042338090221
678898LV00004B/569